Her Frog Prince

SHIRLEY JUMP

In a
Fairy Tale
World

SILHOUETTE *Romance*®

Published by Silhouette Books

America's Publisher of Contemporary Romance

Special thanks and acknowledgment are given to
Shirley Jump for her contribution to the
IN A FAIRY TALE WORLD... series.

To my son, whose fascination with all things slimy and messy has made my life...interesting. You make me laugh more than anyone I've ever known and I wish I could bottle these days with my little boy forever. I love you, messes and all.

SILHOUETTE BOOKS

ISBN 0-373-19746-2

HER FROG PRINCE

This edition published by arrangement with Harlequin Books S.A.

® and TM are trademarks of Harlequin Books S.A., used under license. Trademarks indicated with ® are registered in the United States Patent and Trademark Office, the Canadian Trade Marks Office and in other countries.

Visit Silhouette Books at www.eHarlequin.com

Printed in U.S.A.

"I don't even want to kiss you!"

What had she been thinking? Brad was the wrong man for her. He was a distraction.

A damned good-looking distraction, but still.

He rose, a tall stone sentry in the darkness. "Sure seemed like you wanted to kiss me a second ago."

"You imagined that."

"So if I kissed you right now, you'd hate it?"

"I'd probably slap you." She could lie with the best of them. If he did kiss her, she didn't know what she'd do, but slapping him wasn't anywhere near what her body had in mind.

"Then there's only one thing to do," he said, taking a step closer, to her coming within an inch of her mouth. His gaze flicked from her eyes to her lips and then back to her eyes. "Stay the hell away from each other." His face hardened, then he walked away.

* * *

In a Fairy Tale World...
Six reluctant couples. Five classic love stories.
One matchmaking princess. And time is running out!

Dear Reader,

When you're stuffing the stockings this year remember that Silhouette Romance's December lineup is the perfect complement to candy canes and chocolate! Remind your loved ones—and yourself—of the power of love.

Open your heart to magic with the third installment of IN A FAIRY TALE WORLD..., the miniseries where matchmaking gets a little help from an enchanted princess. In *Her Frog Prince* (SR #1746) Shirley Jump provides a rollicking good read with the antics of two opposites who couldn't be more attracted!

Then meet a couple of heartbreaking cowboys from authors Linda Goodnight and Roxann Delaney. In *The Least Likely Groom* (SR #1747) Linda Goodnight brings us a risk-taking rodeo man who finds himself the recipient of lots of tender loving care—from one very special nurse! And Roxann Delaney pairs a beauty disguised as an ugly duckling with the man most likely to make her smolder, in *The Truth About Plain Jane* (SR #1748).

Last but not least, discover the explosive potential of close proximity as a big-city physician works side by side with a small-town beauty. Is it her wacky ideas that drive him crazy—or his sudden desire to make her his? Find out in *Love Chronicles* (SR #1749) by Lissa Manley.

Watch for more heartwarming titles in the coming year. You don't want to miss a single one!

Happy reading!

Mavis C. Allen
Associate Senior Editor

Please address questions and book requests to:
Silhouette Reader Service
U.S.: 3010 Walden Ave., P.O. Box 1325, Buffalo, NY 14269
Canadian: P.O. Box 609, Fort Erie, Ont. L2A 5X3

SHIRLEY JUMP

has been a writer ever since she learned to read. She sold her first article at the age of eleven and from there, became a reporter and finally a freelance writer. However, she always maintained the dream of writing fiction, too. Since then, she has made a full-time career out of writing, dividing her time between articles, nonfiction books and romance. With a husband, two children and a houseful of pets, inspiration abounds in her life, giving her good fodder for writing and a daily workout for her sense of humor.

The Tale of Her Frog Prince

Once upon a time a princess lost her golden ball down a deep, cool well. She cried as she heard it splash down below. She loved her ball and would give anything to have it rescued. That's when a frog popped up to offer his help.

The frog said, "If you will love me and take me home with you I will bring your ball back."

Thinking the stupid and ugly frog would have to stay in the water, the princess readily agreed. "I promise."

But when the frog retrieved her ball, she hugged it to her chest and ran home, forgetting her promise—until the next day, when the frog came to her house. She slammed the door on him and tried to put him out of her mind. But her father insisted she honor her vow to the frog. Though she was horrified and afraid of the wart-covered frog, she knew she must obey her father.

In her heart, however, she was bitter and angry. When they reached the bedroom she threw him against the wall. "Leave me alone, ugly frog!"

But with her action he became a handsome prince, and she gladly agreed to keep her promise.

From the Brothers Grimm

Prologue

Merry Montrose sat on the deck of *Lady's Delight,* the small cruise boat owned by La Torchere Resort and Spa, and tried not to look miserable. Being an old lady was getting to be, well…old. The curse her godmother Lissa had put on her seven years ago was nearly over, thank goodness. All she had to do was serve as matchmaker to three more couples. So far, she'd put eighteen together; surely, three more should be a cinch. Then she could go back to being twenty-nine-year-old Princess Meredith of Silestia and kiss this old-lady life—and the clunky shoes that came with it—goodbye.

Today, with the horrendous heat, Lissa's spell seemed especially onerous. The air was sticky and thick, the kind of weather that made her wish it would just rain and get it over with.

Merry had gotten on the boat early, to make sure she got the biggest, best and comfiest deck chair. As the resort manager, she should have deferred to a guest, but she did, after all, deserve the good chair, being a member of the elder set. Anyone who looked at her crone-like face and wrinkled skin would think she was at least…well, she didn't want to think about how old she looked. That kind of thought did nothing but depress her.

She glanced down at her vein-mapped legs and age-spotted hands and bit back a sigh. *Soon.* Soon she'd be her young self again and the only wrinkles she'd have would be in her favorite linen suit.

If the heat didn't kill her first. Once the boat got moving, the ocean breeze would cool her down and take her mind off the fact that she had only a few weeks until her thirtieth birthday. If she didn't finagle three more happily-ever-afters, she'd be stuck in this crone body forever.

Merry had been forced to leave the kingdom of Silestia where her family—the *royal* family—lived and relocate to this island in southwest Florida. Once upon a time, she'd been a corporate lawyer. Now, without her résumé, her looks or her money, she'd had to talk herself into this job as resort manager at La Torchere Resort and Spa.

Well, she'd worked a little magic along the way, too. Thank God for that Bessart Family perk. Then Lissa had gone and followed Merry here, getting a job as Lilith Peterson, the concierge. Probably so she could make sure Merry stuck to the conditions of the curse: No telling who she really was. No overt magic. And no return to her old life until she helped along twenty-one happily-ever-afters before she turned thirty. Now Lissa had added a twist—she wanted

Merry to work *this* happy ending without the aid of any magic at all. She'd accused Merry of using it as a crutch. Well, what did Lissa expect? Merry was walking around in the body of a member of the elder set. She needed all the help she could get.

She really needed to get Lissa a hobby so her godmother would stop interfering with Merry's life and quit this lesson-teaching thing. All it did was make her joints ache.

Finally the resort guests began boarding the boat. The last one on—and in three-inch pink Prada heels no less—was Parris Hammond. They'd attended the same college together years ago, back when Merry had been Princess Meredith. Parris had arrived a few weeks ago to help with the resort's charity auction coming up soon and had been a thorn in Merry's existence ever since.

Parris the Princess. Parris the Persnickety. Parris the Annoying.

She'd run out of "P" words, but she had quite a few left from other letters of the alphabet to describe the former debutante.

A lot had changed for Merry in the years since college, but from what she'd seen of Parris lately, not much had changed for—or about—her former classmate.

Parris took a menu from the cook's assistant as she stepped into the boat and immediately let out a sharp sound of disapproval. "I cannot *believe* the catered lunch for this cruise is nothing more than tea and a bunch of garden vegetables between two slices of bread."

The skinny sous-chef looked like he wished he'd

stayed belowdecks instead of greeting passengers. "Ma'am, I assure you, the chef's portabello and artichoke sandwiches are a delight. They'll be quite filling."

"Steak is filling. Lobster is filling. A mushroom, however, is a fungus." Parris shook her head, dug in her purse and tugged out a minirecorder. "Note to self—double-check the menu for the charity auction. If people have empty stomachs, they'll leave with full wallets." She clicked the recorder off, then slid it back into the tiny pink purse dangling from her wrist.

Parris. Still the same as she had been back in college. A major pain in the—

"Can I get you anything, Miss Montrose?"

Merry pressed a handkerchief to her forehead. "Ice water. Extra ice."

"Are you people *ever* going to get this boat moving?" Parris asked, toe tapping against the wooden deck. "We're ten minutes late leaving. I have a meeting with the Phipps-Stovers at three." She parked her hands on her hips and eyed another crew member. "*Well?* Are we leaving or not?"

The mate, who couldn't have been more than nineteen, scuttled back several steps. "Right away, ma'am."

As they got underway, Merry thought if there was anyone she'd known over the years who needed to learn a little humility, it was Parris Hammond. The woman had all the warmth of a porcupine. Somebody ought to teach her a lesson. Maybe put a heel in her pink designer-clad behind when she got too close to the edge. Let some fisherman find her.

Merry smiled and adjusted her sunglasses. The

cruise boat was coming upon a small fishing vessel with a very scruffy looking fellow sitting in it. *Hmm…*

Now *that* was a match she hadn't tried before. Uppity Parris Hammond and a male who spent his days in the dregs of the ocean—a fisherman.

Well, she always *had* liked a challenge. And Parris looked awfully hot. A little cooling off might do them all a world of good.

Chapter One

There it was. Smooth, pink, and gorgeous as hell. Well, gorgeous to him. Everyone else in the world would probably look at the object of Brad Smith's desire and lose their lunch.

Or worse, consider it lunch. In some parts of the world, she'd be considered a delicacy.

Brad was inches away from scooping up another prize squid out of the ocean. It wasn't the species he was seeking, but it was one that could provide a few bonus points when he presented his research to The National Aquatic Research Foundation in two weeks. He needed every boost he could get.

He'd been out here the entire day, and all he had to show for his efforts was one sunburned nose—he'd forgotten the zinc smear on the bridge again—and three dead mackerel, probably thrown back by fishermen who'd accidentally caught them in their nets in their quest for the big-bucks tunas and marlins of Florida's southwest coastline.

The flash of pink went by again, close enough to the surface that Brad could have almost caught it by hand. He dropped his net into the water slowly, hoping he wouldn't startle the creature before he could catch it and study it.

With his other hand, he dipped an oar into the water and pushed the boat to the left. *Gentle. Quiet. Easy now, here she comes again.*

He reached forward and—

Before he could net anything at all, a full orchestra of screams arose from behind him, punctuated by a splash, scaring off the fish, the seagulls and the specimen.

Brad cursed and yanked the empty net into his boat. He wheeled around and saw a pleasure boat tooling away, its wake coming for his little craft like a wave of ants determined to knock over a picnic basket. Caught in the undulating waves behind the retreating *Lady's Delight* was a screeching woman.

Definitely not a mermaid. Too obnoxious sounding to be a whale.

Had to be a tourist.

"Just when I'm about to catch a good one," Brad muttered to Gigi, his shelter-rescued chow, who'd taken her favorite spot on the bow of the inflatable Zodiac boat. "Why do people tour anyway? Why can't they swim in their own pools and stay the hell out of southwest Florida?"

Gigi gave him a soulful look, then lowered her head to her paws.

Brad shouted at the pleasure boat but it didn't turn around. The woman hadn't stopped shrieking, either. He braced his hands on the sides of his eighteen-foot-long boat, holding on as the waves rocked the little craft to the side and back again, each wave lessening in strength.

And still the banshee went on screaming.

Gigi perked up her ears and gave him a bark.

"Oh, you think I should rescue her, huh? Like some knight in shining armor?" Brad looked over the side of his boat, hoping in vain for another flash of pink, but there was nothing. As long as the she-devil was in the water, all marine life was heading for the northern panhandle. If he were smart, so would he. "All right, I'll help her out. But only for the sake of the sea creatures."

Gigi yipped approval and got to her feet. A forty-pound chow in an inflatable research boat wasn't a good combination, but his dog had long ago gotten her sea legs.

Brad tugged up the anchor, yanked the cord on the electric motor, then, with a scowl and several muttered curses, guided the boat to the thrashing woman. He turned off the motor to coast the last few feet toward her so the propeller wouldn't turn her into bait.

Gigi held her ground, balancing on the little wooden seat with all four paws, letting out barks like a canine version of hot-cold as they got closer.

The woman's blond head bobbed in the water, went under, then back up again. A wave dipped beneath her chin.

"You all right?" he called to her.

"Do I—" she spit out a swallow of seawater "—*look* all right to you?"

He tossed the anchor over the opposite side, then

turned back to her, draping his arms over his knees. "What you look is wet."

Beneath the water, he could see long legs and arms making broad strokes as she treaded water with fast, anxious moves, her pink skirt billowing out like the mantle of a jellyfish. If she kept up like that, she'd wear out in five minutes and sink.

Getting a squid into his boat wasn't a problem. Helping a full-grown woman into it was another story. She could easily swamp them and then they'd both be shark snacks. He cast another glance toward the pleasure boat, but it was quickly becoming a dot against the horizon.

She bobbed down, then up again. "Hey, fisher boy! Could you pay attention? There's a drowning—" she spit out more seawater "—woman here!"

Calling him "fisher boy" did *not* induce him to give her a helping hand. "You're not drowning. And you look like you can take care of yourself," he said. "Land's only about three, four miles away."

"Get me out of this water," she said, pronouncing each word with the precision of the Catholic nuns who'd taught him multiplication. "Now."

He didn't move. "Why are you in it?"

She gave him a look that said she thought he was an idiot. "I fell in. Obviously."

"Or did your friends push you in?"

Behind him, Gigi barked. Clearly his chow thought he should stop torturing and start rescuing.

"And what on earth—" more water out "—is that supposed to mean?"

"Well frankly, you don't seem very pleasant."

"Excuse me?"

He had never seen anyone look so haughty while they were treading water. "I'm choosy about who rides in my boat."

She gave him a glare that could have melted a diamond. Her arms started moving even faster at her sides, her legs kicking like hyperactive jackrabbits beneath her. "I'm wet. And late for a meeting. And getting very angry. Before I yank you in the water by your flannel shirt and use your head as a life preserver, would you *please* get me out of here?"

If he'd been raised a jerk, he'd have left her there. Her "please" had sounded about as pleasant as turnips for lunch. Maybe he should leave anyway. Start a new trend of jerkiness. Being a nice guy certainly hadn't gotten him much in life thus far.

But...she did have pretty green eyes. And green happened to be his favorite color. Despite her words, he felt himself relenting. A little. "Gee, when you ask so nicely, how can a guy refuse?"

She gave him another glare. She was really good at those. Must have practiced glaring a lot in finishing school or wherever it was that gave her that attitude.

Brad put out a hand. She caught it and started to haul herself up. "Whoa, not so fast or you'll pull us both in. Do it slow and easy, a little at a time. Here, use the edge of the boat and slide in." He grinned. "Just like landing a marlin."

Her answering scowl told him she didn't like being compared to a hundred-pound prize fish.

It took some effort, and some delicate balancing on his part, but he managed to get her into the boat. When he did, he noticed she was slim yet strong, and only a few inches shorter than his six-foot-two-inch height. Even wet, she was a gorgeous woman, all legs and long blond hair.

She plopped onto the single seat in the center of his boat, minus a shoe. A high-heeled strappy kind of shoe at that. What kind of person wore high heels on a boat ride?

"It took you long enough," she said. With a hand over her eyes to block out the sun, she scanned the horizon for the still departing *Lady's Delight*.

"How'd you fall in anyway?"

She shook her head. "I swear that old woman tripped me when I walked by her. Was she just looking for a lawsuit?"

Brad decided that was a rhetorical question and let it stand unanswered, even though he had a few ready replies.

She pressed a hand to her chest and winced. "You know, you could have broken a rib dragging me in like that."

"You could be more grateful I got you out at all. The sharks are always looking for something to eat."

"Sharks?"

He took in her wide emerald eyes and flushed damp skin. The side of his brain ruled by testosterone contemplated some nibbling of his own, but of a very different kind. *If* he ignored everything that had come out of her mouth thus far, she was a very attractive woman. Maybe she was just having a bad day. A *very* bad day.

And maybe he was too damned nice. Hadn't his mother told him that? More than once in his twenty-nine years of life? Being nice didn't get you ahead.

Didn't get you a plum research position. Didn't get you the notice of the top brass at the Smithsonian.

Being nice got you on a dinghy in the middle of the Gulf of Mexico with a dripping wet, ungrateful woman with more attitude than common sense.

"I'm sorry," she said, letting out a sigh. "Thank you for helping me."

Okay, not so much attitude.

"Apology accepted." He reached behind him for a towel and tossed it her way. Gigi had wisely stayed in her corner of the boat, avoiding the whole thing. Dogs had damned good instincts. "Here. Dry off."

"While I do," she said, waving a manicured hand his way, "you gun the engine and get me over to Torchere Key. If I hurry, I have enough time to change, redo my hair and makeup and look like a human again before I meet with the Phipps-Stovers." She started to rub at her hair with the towel, then paused. "Well, go ahead."

"I don't take orders." Brad picked up the charts beside him and made a few notations about the squid he'd seen, ignoring her. Gigi let out a little bark of support. She didn't much like being bossed around, either.

"Pull that cord thingy, will you?"

Brad dipped a container into the ocean for a water sample, capped it and labeled it with the date and time, using a waterproof marker.

The woman let out a sigh. "What are you doing?"

"Right now? Taking a water sample."

She let out a gust. "Why?"

"I'm looking for something," he replied, answering the water-sample question. Much easier to talk about his work than debate her communication skills. Or lack of them.

"What? Your lunch?"

"Giant squid."

She looked a hell of a lot better speechless. Almost beautiful. Even wet and dripping and half shoeless.

"A…a…giant what?" she finally managed.

"Squid."

She blinked. Several times. "There is such a thing?"

"Well, no one's ever seen a live one, but yes, there is."

She snorted. "Like Bigfoot, I'm sure."

He gave her a glare and dipped his thermometer into the ocean, busying himself with the reading. "They exist."

"Yeah, and so do happy marriages, I hear. I think it's all a bunch of fairy tales people tell their kids to keep them from wandering the streets at night."

He pivoted toward her, the thermometer dangling from his fingers. "What flew up your butt this morning?"

"Excuse me?"

"I didn't fish you out of the water so you could call my research a fairy tale."

"Oh, your *research*." But the tone in her voice said she still didn't believe him.

Gigi got to her feet and in three steps was across the boat and in the woman's face. Standing up for her master, daring the intruder to make fun of the giant squid. Gigi knew. She'd spent enough time on the water to know almost nothing was impossible in the dark blue depths.

"Get that—that—that *creature* away from me."

"No can do. Gigi has a mind of her own. If she doesn't like you, she's going to let you know."

The woman arched a perfectly rounded brow at him. "Your dog's name is *Gigi?*"

Brad crossed his arms over his chest. "Is there anything else about me you want to criticize?"

"Well, actually..." She pointed at his face, then bit her lip and shut up.

"What? Say it."

Gigi continued to hold her ground. Now she was standing up for the giant squid *and* her master.

"Listen," the woman said, pausing, as if apologizing wasn't something she did every day. "We got off on the wrong foot. Let's start over." She extended a shaky, tentative hand past Gigi's side. "I'm Parris Hammond."

He hesitated, then figured the bad mood of the morning was half his fault. No squid, no whale sightings and a wasted day on the boat hadn't put him in a very pleasant frame of mind. "Brad Smith." When he took her hand in his, the cool touch of her skin sent a shock wave through his veins. Like she'd been a power line and he'd been the fool who'd picked it up without wearing rubber shoes.

Except he did have on rubber boots and he didn't feel foolish holding her hand. Not at all.

She withdrew her grasp from his but not before he saw an echo of his own consternation in her eyes. Clearly he wasn't the only one playing with electricity. "Is that short for Bradford?"

"Yeah, but don't ever call me that, not if you want me to answer."

"Why not? I think Bradford sounds...rich."

"Exactly."

"Right." She nodded. "That's good."

"Not in my book." He picked up the chart again and filled in the temperature block.

"Well. Aren't you the enigma?" She went back to drying herself off, toweling down the front of her silky shirt. Brad's attention went from the chart to her, his gaze locked on the movements of the cream-colored terry cloth. It slid along her skin with ease, which made funny things happen in his gut. Her breasts peeked through the damp material of her shirt, giving him a clear image of what she'd look like naked.

The chart slid out of his hands and clattered to the floor of the boat, the pen rolling to the other end. "I, ah, should get you back. You have a meeting with the..."

His eyes met hers and her hand stilled. The air between them grew hot, charged. Her tinted lips parted, but nothing came out for a long second.

"The...the Phipps-Stovers." But she didn't move. In fact, she didn't even seem to breathe.

"You don't want to be late."

Her focus stayed on him. "I'm never late."

"Even for dinner?" Where the hell had that come from?

A tease of a smile lit up her eyes. "Are you asking?"

"Are you accepting?"

She put a hand on her hip. "I'm not accepting until there's a firm offer on the table."

God, the woman was frustrating. He didn't need

these word games. He had enough exasperation looking for a nearly invisible squid. He turned away and
yanked the cord on the engine. The motor gave a little
gurgle, then went silent. "Well, I'm not offering anything."

Apparently, Parris Hammond wasn't used to having dinner invitations rescinded. Out of the corner of
his eye he saw her jerk back, then get busy rubbing
at her hair with the towel, hard enough that he was
afraid she might end up bald. "Good, because I have
a very full schedule."

The motor turned over on the third try and Brad
headed the boat toward the island. "Yeah, me too."

"That giant squid must be very time-consuming."

He wheeled around. "Will you quit with that?"

"I wasn't being sarcastic. Honest. Just making conversation. I mean, what do you say when someone
tells you they hunt squid for a living?" She shud-
dered. "It's so...*gross.*"

"Squid are not gross."

She arched a brow his way.

Brad gunned the engine. Gigi let out a yelp of protest. "Did you know the largest squid ever found
weighed a thousand pounds? And the giant squid's
arms are as thick as a man's thigh? Yet, they've never
been seen alive and are truly one of the biggest mys-
teries of the sea."

"Oh. Fascinating."

He gave her a glance. "You're not impressed."

"I'm impressed someone would know so much
about them." She laid the towel on the bench beside
her. "But why on earth would you want to?"

"I'm a marine biologist. It's my job. Well, it's not

going to be, not in a few weeks. Not if—'' He cut himself off. Why had he told her that? It was more than he'd told anyone in weeks.

"Oh. So what will you do then? Look for dolphins?''

He tossed her a grin. "Start looking for mermaids. I seem to have better luck catching women than squid.''

Then he tilted down his hat, shading his eyes, and concentrated on getting his ''catch'' back to shore before he was tempted to use her for squid bait.

Parris sat in the boat and wondered if she should take that as a compliment or not. Not, she decided. He'd just compared her to a slimy mollusk that caught things with tentacles, for God's sake. That was like being told she had a nice figure by a man with a walrus fetish.

She tried to hold on to the sides of the boat as it skipped across the water, smashing on the waves like a Pinto bottoming out over speed bumps. She should have known better than to wear the Prada shoes for the island cruise. If she was going to lose one, she should have opted for cheaper footwear, something she didn't mind becoming a hermit crab home. She pulled off the remaining shoe and dropped it onto the floor of the boat. She'd go barefoot. At least her pedicure still looked good.

The same could not be said for her Kenneth Cole outfit, though. Salt water and satin apparently didn't co-exist any better than Tom Cruise and Nicole Kidman.

The boat went over a bigger bump, jostling Parris. "Steady there." Brad placed a hand against her back.

A very warm, very large hand. The hand of a man who didn't get manicures every week or spend his days behind a desk, clicking a mouse and sending hundreds of people scurrying to do his bidding.

The ocean whipped by, the motor roared. Sea salt and water sprayed her face. The boat slammed against the water after another big wave and Parris bit back a shriek. "Aren't you going a little fast?" she shouted.

"She may look like an overfilled balloon but she's tough. Built to take about anything."

"I've never been on one of these," Parris said, clutching the seat with a white-knuckled grip. "I don't really like boats. Or the ocean."

"Then why were you on one? In the middle of the Gulf of Mexico?"

"It's my job." She ran a hand through her hair, now sticky with salt and the remains of her hairspray. "This week anyway."

"And next week, what, I can catch your act at the Flamingo Club?"

She tossed him a look over her shoulder. "I don't sing. Or dance."

"Pity, with legs like that." His gaze traveled past the hem of her skirt, down her calves, settling on her ankles for what seemed a very long, very interested time.

"Watch where you're going. Not me."

"Why?"

"So we don't hit a...a..." She looked across the

wide blue expanse of *nothing,* then scowled at him. "Because driving the boat is your job."

"I'm a multifaceted man." He grinned. "I can do two things at once."

"Then drive the boat and think about your squids. Not me."

"Why not?"

"Why not what?"

"Why not think about you?"

"Because I'm not available."

"Married?"

"No."

"Involved?"

"No."

"In a convent?"

"No."

"Good. Me neither." Beneath the brim of his ball cap, his hazel eyes teased her.

She couldn't keep the smile from her face. "I couldn't quite imagine you in a habit."

"Black is not my color." He plucked at the flannel shirt he wore over his faded squid-decorated T-shirt. "I'm more of a plaid guy."

"Yeah, I can see that."

"Oh, I get it," he said, nodding. "You're not available to guys like *me.* Not interested in the scruffy-professor type?"

Her attention roved over the tattered ball cap shading the hazel depths of his eyes, the shaggy beard hiding what she suspected was a strong, square jaw, the cutoff worn flannel that displayed muscular arms yet ballooned around the rest of his well-built chest. If she burned all his clothes, took him to see José, her stylist, and gave a small sacrifice to Estée Lauder, she could *maybe* get Brad Smith looking acceptable enough for public viewing.

Like a man, not a—what did he call himself— scruffy professor. Well, he already looked like a man, just more caveman than cover model. Still, to tell him that to his face would be tactless, and even Parris wasn't direct enough to do that. At least not until they were on solid ground.

"I'm tied up with my career right now. Dating would be a distraction." A lie, but only a grayish one. As soon as her sister Jackie returned from her honeymoon with Steven, her "career" as head of the business would end and she could go back to her life.

If what she had could be considered a life. Lately, she'd had this empty feeling, like she needed more. What more, she couldn't say. Her twenty-seven years of experience had somehow become a cream puff without any filling.

Or maybe she just needed to eat something better than portabellos for lunch.

"A distraction. Uh-huh," he said, clearly not believing her. He shoved the throttle of the boat upward and the little craft lunged forward.

Her heart jerked into her throat and her stomach got lost somewhere ten feet back. "You're going to throw us all out if you keep doing that." Finally the dock for La Torchere came into view. "You can drop me off right here. I'm staying at the resort."

"In the main building or one of the villas?"

She glanced at him. The shaggy beard didn't seem to fit with the appearance of a normal resort visitor.

Maybe there was more to Brad Smith than met the eye. "You've been there?"

The brim of his hat cast his smirk in shadow. "Oh, once or twice." He directed the boat to one of the lower-level docks, brought it up against the fenders and tossed a rope onto the cleat, tying it in a quick, secure loop.

"Well, if you're ever over this way, look me up." Parris scrambled to her feet, trying to maintain her balance in the tilting boat.

"Need some help?"

"I can manage." She stepped off the front end of the boat and put one foot up onto the dock. Before she could get her other leg up, an incoming wave shifted the craft. The boat went one way, she went another.

"Wait...oh! No!" Before she could stop it, she was doing a split worthy of an Olympic bronze medalist.

"Let me—" Brad grabbed her hand. Weaving and wheeling her free arm, Parris pushed off the boat with her other leg, trying to use Brad for leverage to hoist herself up to the dock.

"We should—"

"I wouldn't—"

The two of them tumbled out of the boat and lost their sentences in the water by the pier.

She bobbed up first, then him. "Well, this is fun. *Not.*" Parris spat the hair out of her face and gave him a glower. "Where did you learn how to park?"

"Probably the same place that taught you proper cruise attire."

She swam the few feet over to the ladder on the

end of the pier and climbed up, with Brad following right behind. Gigi barked encouragement from her place in the boat, which was now drifting back toward the dock. "For your information, I was barefoot when I disembarked."

"Who uses words like that?" He stood on the pier, dripping wet and looking even scruffier than he had five minutes ago. "'Disembarked,' for God's sake. Just admit it. You fell in because you didn't listen to me."

Parris parked her fists on her hips. "I fell in because *you* didn't tie up the boat tight enough."

"No. You fell in because you were too stubborn to wait for me to help you."

"You are infuriating! I deal with far less childish people than you in Hollywood."

He arched a brow at her. "*You* work with celebrities?"

"Sometimes. I'm a personal consultant. I help them look, act and sound better." A fib, not an outright lie. She *had* helped her friend Liza get ready for that audition. Liza had nabbed the part, so surely that counted.

Brad started to laugh. And laugh. And laugh until Parris was quite tempted to shove him off the pier and leave him for the sharks. "What's so funny?"

"You. Helping people. What do you do? Bully them?"

"For your information, my clients are *very* happy with my services. I have many success stories." Okay, that one *was* an outright lie. She'd barely worked in the business since her father had turned Hammond Events and Consulting over to her and

Jackie. But she was sure, given the right chance, she *could* do a good job. Probably. "I could even make *you* over. Not that it wouldn't be a challenge, but—"

Brad took a step forward until he was inches away from her. Up close, he didn't look so bad dripping wet. His clothes clung to him, accenting every plane and muscle. She'd been wrong about his lack of manliness. If anything, he was more male than any man she'd ever known. Too bad he drove her up a wall.

He pointed at her chest. "*You* are the most aggravating woman I have ever met."

Give a man some beauty tips and he turns on you. "And you have all the personality of a wolverine."

He glowered at her. She glowered back.

Brad opened his mouth to speak again, but Parris wasn't going to listen to another personal attack. She'd had quite enough of that, thank you very much. She thrust out her arms and shoved him as hard as she could.

Too late, the words he'd started to speak permeated the anger in her mind and she realized he'd been saying he was sorry. Before she could do anything to stop it, he stumbled back, arms wheeling, and fell into the Gulf.

Again.

Whoops. Not the best way to repay him for rescuing her.

Parris peeked over the pier and caught Brad's reddened face and narrowed eyes. His ball cap had fallen off his head and was floating away, just out of reach.

He didn't seem sorry anymore. In fact, he looked pretty mad. From the boat, Gigi let out several barks.

"Do you, ah, need some help getting out of there?"

"Not from you!" He started swimming for the ladder.

"Listen, I'm really sorry. I acted without thinking. If there's any way I can ever make it up to you—"

His answering glare told her he wasn't interested in any favors. Probably better to leave. She had a feeling he didn't want her within ten feet of him right now.

"Well, thanks for the ride. And hey, look at the bright side," Parris said. "If a squid happens by, you'll be in the right place!"

Chapter Two

Brad Smith wasn't a fisherman, but he was one of the few men Merry figured could stand toe-to-toe with Parris and win. She closed her magical cell phone, blessing the powers that allowed her to keep tabs on her matchmaking efforts from afar, and settled back in the deck chair.

Getting Parris a happy ending wasn't an impossible task. But it wasn't going to be an easy one, either. Still, she'd done quite well with Jackie and Steven, and Ruthie and Diego, who would be celebrating their marriage soon. Maybe this wasn't out of her reach.

And maybe Miss Prissy Parris could learn a lesson or two about life, love and acceptance out of the whole thing. A real happy ending.

Yes, Bradford Smith and Parris Hammond. It could work. Right?

Brad stepped out of the shower and swiped the steam off the mirror. He stared at the reflection before him and realized a hard, sad truth. Parris Hammond had a point. One he'd done a good job of ignoring until she'd gone and brought it up.

There wasn't a hell of a lot of difference between Brad the sea-roughened marine biologist and Brad the cleaned-up version. He still looked like something that had washed up at low tide with the kelp and dead crabs.

Aw, hell. The meeting with the research foundation was only ten days away. His research was good and solid, the specimens he'd collected well preserved, but the biologist...well, Brad had to admit he'd gotten a little rough around the edges lately.

He rubbed his beard. Okay, a lot. Jeez, no wonder Parris Hammond had recoiled from him like a third-grader from brussels sprouts.

Problem was, Brad wasn't the kind of guy who cared a hell of a lot about appearances. His own or other people's. Hell, he worked with squid all day. That alone was a clue to his regard for the company he kept. If there was an uglier animal on the planet, he'd yet to see it. But it had been enough to garner a comment from Parris, so maybe it was time he did something about himself.

He left the bathroom of the studio apartment connected to his research offices and went into the main lab. Jerry, his assistant, and the only one he could still afford to pay now that his first grant had just about run out, sat at the counter, making notations in the log.

"Jerry, tell me the truth. You think I need a little help in the, ah, appearance department?" Brad asked.

Jerry looked up from his work, cast a quick glance at Brad's T-shirt and khakis and shrugged. "The squid don't care what you look like and neither do I. Or are you asking me for some other reason?"

"Yeah. That research foundation thing. If I go in there, looking like this, I doubt they'll take me seriously."

The fish didn't care if he showed up in a tux and tails or a duck costume when he went out to do his research. But if he went into the meeting with The National Aquatic Research Foundation looking like something Jacques Cousteau had dragged out of the depths, he had zero chance of getting that grant and continuing his funding. If there was anything a committee liked, it was a good-looking scientist they could parade in front of the media. That and someone who sounded like they were professional, on the ball—and ahead of the research curve.

"Well," Jerry said, running a hand through his red hair. "You *could* use a new look."

"What do you suggest? I chuck my wardrobe and go shopping for some black silk pants and bow ties?"

"Uh, I dunno. I'm not exactly the one to ask." Jerry patted the front of his Real Men Belch T-shirt.

"I see your point."

"What about your mom? Isn't that the kind of thing moms live for? To dress up their kids like their own personal Barbie dolls?"

Brad got to his feet and poured himself a cup of coffee from the pot on the counter. After sitting there in a hot pot all day, the liquid had metamorphosed into something dark as night and almost unrecognizable as java. "Calling my mother is not a good idea."

"That's right. She's not exactly the president of your squid fan club, is she?"

Asking his mother for advice would be inviting her opinion, something Brad had learned long ago wasn't in his best interests. "Right now, my mother is all wrapped up in the charity auction at La Torchere. She's raising funds for the aquarium she wants to build."

"Well, that's support for what you do, isn't it?"

"Building cages for sea life instead of supporting the study of them in the wild? No, I wouldn't call it support." Brad took a long gulp of coffee, ignoring the bitter taste. "All she wants me to do is serve on the Board of Directors. She doesn't want me actually getting my hands dirty."

Jerry put on a bright face, clearly seeing Brad's mother was a sore point to be dropped. "Then what you need, my friend, is a girl. Preferably one with style." Jerry tapped his chin with a pen. "Do we know any of those? Not Lucy. She does that thing with eating her hair. Mary's okay, but I'm not sure she can see with those glasses. And Kitty is always wearing those red socks with purple shorts. Even *I* know your socks shouldn't be brighter than your shorts." Jerry put up a finger. "Wait a minute. There's Susan. She's gorgeous, well acquainted with whatever it is they talk about in those fashion magazines, and—"

"My ex-fiancé."

"I forgot that detail. Guess you don't want to call her for help?"

"I believe she's on her honeymoon right now. With husband number two."

"Oh. Yeah. Timing might be bad." Jerry sighed. "Well, that's the end of my list of people who know how to mix and match." He spun a formaldehyde-filled jar of preserved squid on the counter. "I don't think these guys are going to be any help. You're on your own, buddy."

"I know a woman," Brad said finally. "And she wears that designer stuff you see in the magazines."

"Jackpot! Where'd you meet her?"

"She, ah, sort of climbed into my boat when I was out there today."

Jerry looked at him askance. "Uh-huh. A beautiful woman just happened to climb out of the sea and into your boat. Like a mermaid. Next you'll be telling me they're running unicorns at the horse track."

"She fell off *Lady's Delight*. You know, the boat for the resort? I was there, so I picked her up."

"Was she cute?"

"I wouldn't call her cute, but rather…" He thought a minute. "Sassy."

Jerry grinned. "Sounds interesting."

"She was. In a way."

"So, you gonna call her?"

Brad rubbed at his chin again. The shoe Parris had left in his boat sat on the back counter, like the proverbial glass slipper waiting to be fitted on the right foot. "Yeah. Maybe make a personal visit."

Jerry grabbed a research journal, flipped to a blank page and took up a pencil. "Wait, let me make a note of this." He scribbled the date at the top, then the time.

"What are you doing?"

"A minor miracle is happening in front of my eyes, I thought I'd document it for posterity."

"Minor miracle?"

"Workaholic Brad is calling a woman for a date. Hey, you might actually have something besides squid on your mind for once."

"I am not calling her for a date. More a—" he glanced again at the pink sandal "—consultation."

Jerry tossed the journal and pencil to the side, then sat back down on the stool. "You spoil all my fun. How's a guy going to live vicariously if you don't live at all?"

Parris took a deep breath and pressed a hand to her hair, stopping outside The Banyan Room to look in the mirror and check for the twentieth time that no seaweed or trace of her ocean adventure remained. Everything was as it should be. After a quick shower and change of clothes, She looked capable. Smart. Like she could handle this.

In other words, like a fairy tale. Truth was, Parris wasn't sure she *could* handle this. But she wanted to. Wanted to prove she could.

When her younger sister Jackie had left her in charge of planning and hosting this huge charity auction worth hundreds of thousands of dollars to go off to marry Steven, Parris had, at first, felt angry and put upon. Then, as the days passed, she'd begun to feel energized by the challenge. As a woman who'd never taken the opportunity to be anything more than a society princess, this was new ground.

Exciting ground. And yet, at the same time, terrifying territory because her footing was unsure. The auction was the first big event for Hammond Events and Consulting, the company their father had given them as a sort of test and as his convoluted way of bringing his two daughters together.

With Jackie living among the cow patties and horseflies in connubial bliss at Steven's Florida ranch while Parris did all the auction work, togetherness wasn't happening. And with all the donor problems they'd had in recent weeks, Parris wasn't so sure the auction was happening, either. She *wanted* this to work out, more now than ever. In the past few weeks, she'd seen the opportunity the auction presented to make something of her life. Of herself.

Toward that goal, she had to convince the Phipps-Stovers to make a donation. She squared her shoulders, flicked a piece of lint off her suit and took in a breath.

Merry Montrose, the resort's manager, came up to her before Parris could enter the restaurant. "How are you, Miss Hammond? I heard about your awful accident."

Parris bit back the momentary thought that Merry had somehow been the one doing the tripping this afternoon. "I'm fine. Just surprised no one heard me fall in or turned around when I started screaming."

"Oh, you know how those excursion boats are. So noisy. And at my age, the hearing's not so good."

Merry leaned closer, her blue-violet eyes zeroing in on Parris's. When she was younger, she must have been gorgeous, Parris decided.

"I heard you were rescued."

"There was a man in a boat who fished me out."

"A true knight in shining armor?"

"I wouldn't call him that." She didn't know what she'd call Brad Smith, but "knight" wasn't the word that came to mind. "I don't believe in those kinds of things anyway."

"What kinds of things?"

Oh God. The woman was going to stand here all day and delay Parris from her meeting. But because the auction was being held at the resort, Parris couldn't afford to offend the manager.

"Fairy tales," Parris said curtly, trying her best to end the conversation. "All the Brothers Grimm did was warp a lot of impressionable young minds."

"Do I detect some bitterness?"

Nosy old woman. Parris didn't answer. She wasn't about to get into a conversation about her personal life with the resort manager. Lately the woman had seemed to be quite the busybody, as if she had some kind of personal stake in Parris's life. Maybe she fancied herself a matchmaker. Parris didn't need help from her to find Mr. Right. She didn't even have time for Mr. Right. She had a career to build, not a relationship to find.

Merry had turned and was looking through the oval glass in the doors that led into The Banyan Room. "There's a happy ending in there."

Parris peered through the glass, too. Inside, the Phipps-Stovers were sitting at a table for four by the fireplace, sipping champagne and eating the strawberry-topped cheesecake Parris had arranged as a special treat. Brian Phipps-Stover fed his wife a bit of cheesecake. Joyce giggled as she slipped the bite into her mouth.

God save Parris from newlyweds.

Didn't they know what was going to happen three weeks, three months, three years—maybe even three hours—from now? The little charade of happiness would stop and everyone would show their true ugly colors, turning happily-ever-after into a-nightmare-a-day.

Parris had watched her parents' marriage self-destruct. She'd seen her own fall apart before she'd even come within fifty feet of the altar. Happy endings were a con perpetrated by couples who pretended to live in harmony while they tucked the fights over bills and in-laws out of sight when company arrived.

"Everyone can have a happy ending," Merry said, as if reading Parris's mind.

"All I want is a happy auction." Parris excused herself, then pushed on the doors and entered the upscale restaurant. She glanced at her watch. Only three minutes late. If she hadn't had that conversation with Merry, she would have been on time.

Parris pasted on a smile and crossed to the Phipps-Stovers, trying to stomach the endearments of "pookie" and "truffle lips" that echoed between them as they finished off the last of the cheesecake.

"Hello, Mr. and Mrs. Phipps-Stover. It's a pleasure to meet you in person," Parris said, extending her hand. "I'm Parris Hammond, co-owner of Hammond Events and Consulting. I believe you've already talked with my sister Jackie."

Both Phipps-Stovers rose and greeted her in turn. "Is that Miss Hammond or Mrs.?" Joyce asked.

"Miss. I'm afraid I haven't been as lucky as you." Parris put a broader smile on her face as all three of them sat down. "I've yet to find a man who suits my taste."

"Luck hasn't much to do with marriage," Brian said, spearing a strawberry with his dessert fork. "I've had better luck in Vegas."

Joyce pursed her lips and cast him a sour look but didn't say anything.

"First, I wanted to thank you for your support of the Victoria Catherine Smith Memorial Aquarium Fund," Parris said. "It's a wonderful cause and your donation will enable us to showcase the wonderful marine life in this area for everyone to see."

"I like fish. They entertain me." Brian shrugged, popped the strawberry in his mouth, then took a sip from the flute of champagne.

"Darling, you sip the champagne, then bite the strawberry," Joyce said. "That provides the maximum epicurean effect."

"If I do that, pookie, I get seeds stuck in my teeth. I eat the berry first and then wash it down with champagne."

Joyce's smile strained against her cheeks. "Really darling, people will think you're uncouth if you do that."

Brian's gaze narrowed. He put down his fork and crossed his arms over his chest. "People? Or just you?"

Uh-oh. The bloom was already off the Phipps-Stover rose. Their union more resembled a bunch of thorns covered with a few lingering petals.

"Let's discuss what you're donating to the auction," Parris said, interjecting a change of subject before the strawberries became the beginning of a food fight.

The Phipps-Stovers recovered their manners from somewhere off the floor and slipped back into proper society mode. Brian reached into the breast pocket of his suit and withdrew a checkbook. "If you'll just give me a pen—"

"Oh no, darling." Joyce laughed. "We aren't writing a check. That's so…impersonal. I thought we'd donate a piece of art."

"What piece of art?"

"That painting in the parlor. The one over the fireplace."

"My great-aunt painted that."

"Darling, it's just a bit risqué for our tastes, don't you think? I mean, all those orchids and lilies. It's…well, it doesn't send the right message."

"Are you trying to say my aunt's painting is the equivalent of an HBO special?" He was half out of his seat.

Oh God. This wasn't going well at all. Parris had no idea what to do. The only event planning she'd ever done was RSVPing to a party invitation. She had to save the situation. But how?

"Your aunt was institutionalized, dear. For her overabundance of men." Joyce put on a tight smile and gritted her teeth. "Her paintings reflected her…needs, shall we say? And they certainly are the talk of the town. They'd fetch quite the price."

"My great-aunt was a Stover. That makes her someone to be respected, not gossiped about."

It looked like the Phipps-Stovers were about to come to blows. Parris wished for the hundredth time that Jackie was there to help her. But no, Jackie had to go off and get married. Granted, Jackie deserved a happy life, but still, couldn't it have waited until after the auction was over?

"I'm sure we can work it—" Parris began.

Brian got to his feet. "I'm through with this. Forget the whole thing."

"Please stay. I'm sure we can—"

Joyce rose as well. "I'm not staying, either. In fact, I'm not even staying on the island."

"Good. There'll be more room on the beach, considering all you do is take up sand and bake yourself to a crisp."

Joyce let out an indignant gasp. "I do not!"

"Before you know it, you'll look as old and wrinkled as that sculpture your grandmother dumped on us."

Joyce put a hand over her gaping mouth. "I cannot believe you said that. That marble bust of Great-Grandfather Phipps is an heirloom. A piece of history."

"It's a piece of—"

"There's an easy way to settle this," said a male voice Parris had hoped she wouldn't hear again.

She spun around and found Brad Smith standing a few feet away, a small bag in one hand. He was freshly showered and in a different T-shirt, but he still looked more like a California college student than a grown-up.

Both the Phipps-Stovers had stopped arguing, though. Either they were waiting with bated breath for Brad's solution or they'd been stunned into silence by the appearance of a beach bum in The Banyan Room.

Brad dug into his pocket and tossed a quarter at them. Brian caught it in his right hand. ''There's your solution,'' Brad said.

''Flip a coin?'' Joyce looked horrified.

''It's a true fifty-fifty chance. And the best way to end a battle between two people who both want to be right.''

''We're not battling…exactly.'' Joyce said.

''We're newlyweds,'' Brian added.

''That explains everything,'' Brad said with a smile. ''Try it. You don't really want to fight, do you?''

Joyce looked at Brian. Brian looked at Joyce. Then he shrugged. ''Why not? I'm a betting man.'' He jiggled the coin in his hand. ''Call it, babycakes.''

She pursed her lips, let out a sigh. ''Heads.''

Brian tossed the quarter into the air, caught it and slapped it onto the back of his hand. Before revealing the coin's position, he paused. ''Whatever this is, we abide by it. I don't want to fight with you anymore, honeybunny.''

''Oh, me either.'' Joyce nodded.

Brian lifted his right palm. ''You win.''

''No, we both win, sweetums.'' Joyce grasped his arm and gave her husband a loud, smacking kiss on the cheek.

And just like that, the storm between the Phipps-Stovers had passed. ''We'll donate the painting,'' Brian said. ''Someone else will surely love it as much as I do.''

"And then we'll go shopping for something together. Something that's just us," Joyce said.

"Oh, truffle lips, you're so perfect."

Happiness had been restored. Within a few minutes, the Phipps-Stovers had completed the paperwork for their donation and had left the restaurant, snuggled once again in newlywed bliss. Brad and Parris wandered out of The Banyan Room and onto the veranda.

"Now you owe me twice," Brad said, smiling at her. "Actually, three times." He handed her the bag.

When he smiled, his eyes lit up and something traveled between them, like a connection of energy. How could that be? She'd known the man, what, forty minutes, and spent most of that time dripping wet and mad as hell at him.

"What's this?" she asked.

"Your glass slipper, Cinderella. You left it in my boat."

She felt her face flush. For the briefest of seconds, she had felt like she was in a fairy tale. Who was she kidding? She was an heiress and he was a *squid* hunter. That was fairy-tale *hell*. "Thanks," she said. "Again."

"I want more than a little gratitude."

"What…money? Are you some mercenary rescuer who goes looking for damsels in distress?"

He cocked his head, considering that for a minute. "If I could find a way to make it lucrative, I might. Make my time on the ocean a little more productive."

"I'm not paying you for rescuing me." She raised her chin. "It's the deed of a good citizen. And you look like…"

"Like what?"

"Well, like you *could be* a good citizen." The last thing she wanted to be was indebted to him. That meant spending time with Brad Smith. A man like him—who drove her crazy and sent her thoughts careening into wild, impossible corners—wasn't what she needed right now.

"If I cleaned up a bit. Put on a tie, you mean?"

"Well…" She glanced at his T-shirt. Plain, unadorned, no beer-swilling logo or sea life on it. "Yeah."

"Good."

"Good?"

"You said you're available for personal consultations. And I want one."

Oh no. No way. She knew what he meant. It wasn't a "consultation" at all. He wanted some kind of sex thing, she was sure. No one hired her. She didn't have any experience. "Is this some weird way of asking me out on a date? Because—"

"I want to hire you."

"Hire me?" She blinked. "As in pay me money to help you with a project?"

"Yeah, is that so unusual? I mean, that is what you do in your business, right?"

"Oh yeah." She let out a hiccup of a laugh. "All the time." At least all the time in the past few weeks. Before that, the only thing she'd been good at was signing her name on charge-card receipts.

"Good. Then you can help me."

"Help you with what?"

He patted his chest. "Become more of a tie guy."

She didn't believe him for a second. Most men

were happy with the way they looked and had a heart attack if a woman changed the brand of athletic socks they wore. There was no way this guy was for real. He wanted something else. Something definitely not involving "consulting."

Besides, he didn't look like the kind of guy who could afford her fee, whatever it might be, since this was her first real customer, other than organizing the auction for Victoria Smith. "And how were you planning on paying me?"

"I already paid in advance. With the rescue in the water and by helping that couple. I'm low on cash otherwise."

Parris held the stack of auction papers close to her chest. There were a hundred details yet to take care of before the auction on Saturday, just four days away. With Jackie gone, she couldn't afford to lose her focus, not for a second. If there was anything Brad Smith would surely make her do, it was lose her focus. Even if he was sincere about hiring her—which she couldn't imagine he was since he didn't need a tie to pull up squids—she didn't have time for him. "I can't right now. I'm too busy with the auction."

"Let me guess. The auction to benefit the Victoria Catherine Smith Memorial Aquarium, right?"

"You've heard about it?"

"Often." Brad scowled. Apparently he hadn't heard anything good. Was her PR campaign that bad? "I can see why that might be more…demanding."

"Yes, it is. So, you understand why I can't take you on right now." There. She had a valid excuse not to get involved with him, whether she owed him a favor or not. She'd write him an IOU and hope he'd forget about it.

He took a step forward, invading her space, forcing her to deal with him. "No, I don't. But if you say you can't, I intend to find a way around that."

A soft breeze whispered through the veranda, lifting her hair. Resort guests came and went, drifting down to the beach or back up to their rooms for a nap.

"There is no way around that, Mr. Smith. If I say I'm busy, I am. My apologies." She started flipping through the paperwork, hoping she looked too consumed to deal with him.

He gave a short nod, then stepped back. "Fine."

"Thank you again for your help. And, for my shoe." There. She sounded businesslike. She'd made it clear this transaction was over. She owed him nothing, especially not his weird idea of a date.

"Don't mention it." His voice had gone cold. He pivoted on his heel and left the veranda.

She glanced up from her papers and watched him walk away, tall and purposeful. A good-looking man beneath all of that…scruffy professor.

She'd gotten what she wanted. So why did she feel a rush of disappointment? Parris shook her head, determined to ignore it and go back to the auction details.

But the paperwork swam in front of her eyes and the lists became a jumbled mess, filled with images of Brad Smith.

She blinked until her vision cleared. The last thing she needed was a squid researcher who thought he could channel Prince Charming.

Chapter Three

Well, that hadn't gone well. Brad left the resort, heading around the island to his little research building tucked on the other side. There were no people there, except for Jerry, who knew when to leave Brad alone. His life was as close to being a hermit as a man could get without having to live in a cave.

It suited Brad just fine, particularly if being among the human race meant dealing with women like Parris. Thanks to Susan, he'd learned his lesson already about the risks of getting involved with uppity women and he had no desire to repeat it.

Besides, Parris infuriated him. Drove him completely insane. Made him—

Want to grab her and kiss her until these crazy feelings churning inside him stopped.

And if anyone needed to be kissed until she got rid of her attitude, it was Parris Hammond.

Brad decided to put her out of his mind but found

it was easier said than done. He went to bed that night and his dreams were filled with a teasing mermaid with blond hair and green eyes.

When his phone rang at the crack of dawn the next morning, he reached for it blindly, realizing he'd had almost no sleep the night before. He mumbled a greeting into the receiver.

"Hello, darling," his mother said.

"Mother. What a surprise." Victoria Catherine Smith usually only called him when she had something to complain about or had to make an obligatory holiday greeting.

"I wondered if…" Her voice trailed off, sounding uncertain. Impossible. His mother was never uncertain about anything. She had opinions and she voiced them. Especially about her son's "bad" career choices.

"Wondered what?"

"Oh, nothing." Her voice had resumed its usual briskness. He must have imagined the moment of vulnerability. "I'll be coming down from Boston soon, for the auction on Saturday night to benefit my aquarium. It's going to be a wonderful place when it's built. You should be a part of that, starting with the auction. You will be there, won't you?"

"I'm busy with my research, Mother."

She let out a gust. "The fish again?"

"Squid. I research giant squid."

"Eww. That's even worse. You know, you're a brilliant man. You could come back to Massachusetts, work in the family—"

"Don't start that again, Mother."

"Bradford, how can you be happy handling worms and dead fish all day?"

"I'm in my element. You should see me." He almost laughed at the irony of the statement, considering he was wearing a Squid Are Just Misunderstood Octopuses T-shirt.

"I've never seen what attracted you to that career."

"That's part of the problem."

"The aquarium could be such an opportunity for you—"

"To sit at a desk all day?"

"It would get you out of those awful boats."

"I love those boats, Mother, and my job. I'm not looking for another one."

"Well, I'll have an invitation waiting for you all the same. And please wear a suit. I know you have several from Brooks Brothers. I mailed them to you myself."

The thought of a suit made him feel suffocated. The three pieces represented everything he'd run from when he'd left the Smith name—and its fortune—behind. "I'll try." He wasn't going to make a promise he couldn't keep.

His thoughts drifted again to Parris Hammond, to his request that she help him become more of a tie guy. He needed a tux for the dinner and meeting with the grant committee. A tux he didn't have. And he needed something else—a feeling of comfort while wearing the ridiculous penguin suit. He'd spent too many years in shorts and T-shirts, avoiding everything corporate. On the water, yes, he was, as he'd said, in his element. Out of it, he was like a fish—

flopping and gasping for air, not knowing what the hell to do with himself.

He had the feeling Parris Hammond, despite how insane she made him feel, held the key to helping him ease his transition back into civilized society. Cro-Magnon man gets dressed up and comes to dinner.

His mother let out a dissatisfied sigh. "I suppose I should let you get back to your octopuses."

"Squid."

"Whichever. They're both disgusting."

"Then why are you sponsoring an aquarium?"

"I don't intend to actually *look* at the things inside the tanks, Bradford. It's a legacy."

Brad flopped against his pillows and bit back his first response. And his second. "I need to go, Mother. It's almost time for me to catch a whaling boat."

"I'll see you in a few days, dear."

He hung up, then rolled out of bed. He'd focus on squid and sperm whales. Preferably male ones only.

Because the women in his life were far too much trouble.

Merry closed her magic cell phone and let out a sigh. The reception had been fuzzy. The silly thing seemed to be on the fritz again, but it didn't matter. The brief review of yesterday's interactions between Brad and Parris was enough to tell her that her current matchmaking project wasn't getting off to a good start.

She'd heard Brad mention just now that he was getting ready to go off on a whaling boat. That seemed like a nice, quiet location. Away from the resort and all the tensions of the auction. If she could find a way to get Parris out there, too, maybe Merry could still salvage—or goodness, create at least—something between the two of them.

Merry hurried out of her private villa and up to the main resort building. Parris was already at the front desk, barking orders at the clerk who had made the mistake of getting a message wrong.

Parris, clad once again in something designer, rubbed at her temples. "I'm sorry," she said. "I just had a donor call and change their item at the last minute, the brochures were a mess that took a whole day to straighten out and the company supplying the thank-you gifts just sent me two hundred 'It's a Boy' cardboard storks instead of the marble desk clocks I ordered. Nothing's going right with this auction and I'm taking it out on you."

Parris being nice? Parris apologizing? Well, with that kind of miracle happening before her eyes, Merry had renewed hope she could make this couple work.

"Mr. Kingman told me to give this to you," the clerk said. "It's your invitation to brunch on the Kingman yacht." He handed Parris a cream-colored envelope.

Merry recognized the name. The Kingmans were wealthy philanthropists who gave to almost every cause that involved marine life. They vacationed often at the resort, enjoying the privacy of the beach and the abundance of aquatic animals in the area. Parris would have no trouble securing a donation from them. Which meant—

If she missed the brunch, it wouldn't be too big of a hardship.

Hmm. Seemed a little magic was in order to help

the Brad and Parris match-up, especially since Parris still owed him a favor. Merry took a quick glance around. Her godmother Lissa would never approve of her using magic in such a public place. But Merry was getting desperate. She'd been cursed to walk as an old woman long enough. Just a few more couples and she could go back to her youthful life.

Desperate times—and desperate wrinkles—called for desperate measures.

Just as Parris withdrew the invitation to the brunch, Merry waved her index finger in a little loop. "Magic pen, write again," she whispered, "and send her on a trip with a scruffy gentleman."

And so it was done. Merry slipped off into the shadows. She sure hoped Parris had her sea legs on today. In those shoes, she was going to need them.

"This can't be right," Parris muttered. She pulled the invitation out of her Liz Claiborne purse and looked at it again. It still said Dock Four and named *Tabitha's Curse* as the boat she was supposed to board. The only boat she saw parked at Dock Four looked about as much like a luxury yacht as a vulture looked like a swan.

"I'm going back to the resort," she said to herself. But as she took a step to turn back, a thick fog swirled up around her. The white mist blocked her vision, knocking her perception off.

She hesitated on the dock. Was she moving toward the boat? Or away from it?

"Right this way, miss," said a man's voice. "Your boat is leaving soon." She felt his guiding hand, though she couldn't see him through the heavy fog.

She didn't want to miss the Kingman boat—or the Kingman donation opportunity—so she trusted the invisible stranger to guide her.

A moment later, Parris was walking up the gangplank. She heard water slapping against the wooden sides, felt the rocking of the craft in the tiny wakes created within the bay by other boats, heard the shouts of the crew as they were ordered to "cast off" and "make way."

But she still couldn't see a damned thing. What kind of fog was this?

By touch, Parris managed to find a railing. Maybe if she stayed here until the boat was farther from the island, the fog would clear enough for her to make her way belowdecks to the Kingmans. She didn't want to chance it now, not in her Ralph Lauren sandals. They were a perfect match to the sleeveless black-and-white-diagonal-patterned dress she'd chosen, but they weren't exactly seaworthy.

Five minutes passed. Ten. Fifteen. And still, the fog remained, more like soup than clouds. Above her, she could see the sun, a fuzzy orange circle trying to break through. She caught a whiff of something very unsavory. Lord, must be the boat next to them or the water in the bay. She hoped they were away from it soon.

"Parris? What are you doing here?"

She turned toward the voice. The fog parted a little, like an opening in a curtain, allowing Parris to see she was nose-to-nose with Brad Smith. "What are *you* doing on the Kingmans' boat?"

"The Kingmans?" Brad laughed. "They don't

own this heap. They may like aquatic life, but this is a bit too rustic for them.''

''What are you talking about?'' Then, as she said the words, the rest of the fog lifted, as if someone had waved a magic brush and whisked it all away.

Oh God. Parris's jaw dropped open. Thick ropes coiled on the weather-beaten wooden decks. A huge cranelike thing sat in the middle of the bow. The pilothouse sported peeling white paint and windows peppered with salt spray.

Worse than the ragged, dirty, jumbled appearance was the smell. Now that her eyes could connect with her location, her nose made the final link.

Dead, rotted fish. The odor was more disgusting than anything she'd ever smelled in her life. A few feet away, a man in a yellow raincoat hosed off the deck, ostensibly trying to wash it away. It didn't seem to be working.

Brad swept his arm in a semicircle, indicating their conveyance. ''This is *Tabitha's Curse,* a whaling boat.''

Tabitha must have done something horrible to be cursed with *this* namesake.

''Whaling boat?'' The sick feeling in the pit of her stomach grew in intensity.

''Yeah. I'm surprised to see you on it. I had no idea you loved sperm whales.'' He grinned.

''I don't. I'm not even supposed to be here.'' She fished the invitation out of her purse. ''It says, 'The Kingman Yacht for brunch.' See?'' She thrust it at him and outlined the words with her finger.

''I can read.'' Brad pushed the paper away, scowling. ''I may look dumb, but I'm not.''

"I never said you were."

He shook his head. "Sometimes, Parris, you don't need to speak."

"What's that supposed to mean?"

"I've seen the way you look at me. Like I'm an idiot because I can't coordinate a shirt with a pair of pants. I spend my days on boats like this one." He indicated the whaling boat. "A suit would be a bit out of place."

Brad looked far from scruffy today. He had on a navy tank top and khaki shorts, both of which set off his tan and showed that beneath everything, he was a man.

A very muscular man. A very...handsome man.

She swallowed and took a step back, refusing to say that to him. To acknowledge those feelings, to him or herself. She was *not* going down that road today. She was already on the wrong boat. No need to make any more wrong turns. "They have to turn the boat around. Now."

"No can do."

"I can't miss the Kingmans' brunch. They're donating to the auction."

"And I can't miss my whale. He's going to take me to the squids." Brad's focus went to the ocean. "I hope."

"I *cannot* spend my day on this heap."

He turned and looked at her, a slow glance that swept her from head to toe. "Not in those shoes, you can't."

"Not in any shoes, not in any outfit," Parris said, infuriated that her cheeks were hot, her traitorous body pleased with his perusal. "We have to turn around."

"Sorry." He grinned. "You're stuck with me. Déjà vu."

"Not for long." She dug in her purse, yanked out her cell phone and flipped it open. A blank, black face greeted her. No power. In all the rush with the auction in the past couple of days, she'd forgotten to charge it. She muttered a curse under her breath. "Can this day get any worse?"

"Sure it can. But it can also get better. You're stuck here, Parris. So why not enjoy it?"

She took a look around the battered, stinky decks. "I don't think so."

Brad shrugged. "Suit yourself." Then he walked away, clambering up the steps to the pilothouse.

There was only one solution. Mutiny.

A little over an hour later, Brad found Parris below-decks, clutching the tabletop as if it were an oak tree in a hurricane. "Are you going to sit there and sulk all day?"

She swung her head toward him in a slow semi-circle. Her skin had gone ashen, nearly green. She had her lips pursed together tightly, as if the mere act of speaking would send her stomach over the edge.

He couldn't keep from smiling. From his perpetual station by the coffeepot, Jerry sent Brad a grin and arched his brow, silently questioning who the woman was. Brad didn't elaborate. He did, however, bite back the urge to tell Parris she deserved a little nausea for the way she'd treated him. "Ocean a little rough for you?"

She scowled. "Let me die alone, please."

Brad laughed and took her arm, tugging her gently to her feet. "Come on. You're not going to get better staying down here."

"I don't want to get better. I want to die." She pressed a hand to her stomach.

"Trust me."

She gave him a glance that told him how much she trusted him. She must have felt worse than she looked, though, because she went along with him, limp as a damp towel. He helped her up the ladder, those ridiculous shoes catching on the holes in the aluminum treads.

Brad put out a hand to steady her. He connected with her lithe waist and she moved, taking a step. The silky fabric of her dress shifted against her side, rubbing against his palm, as smooth as gliding along her bare skin.

Brad missed the next step and nearly fell down the ladder. Keep a little distance. A much better plan.

Yeah, except the more distance he had, the more he noticed the shapely curve of her backside, the heart-shaped flex of her calves, the smooth tightness of her thighs.

The boat rocked over a wave and Parris swayed into his arms. A burst of heat exploded in his chest. "Steady there," he told himself more than her. Gigi took one look at them, bumping into each other like two boats that couldn't stay on course, and padded off to the sunny bow.

"I am steady." She jerked forward and went back to climbing the ladder, putting a lot more distance between them than before.

Hmm. Maybe the impervious Parris wasn't so immune to him after all.

He shook his head. He was here to do research. Important data that he needed to gather today if he was going to have any hope of wowing the research foundation in a week. Since he hadn't chosen the mating habits of marine biologists with uppity society women as his subject, he needed to refocus on whales and squid.

Not Parris and those awesome legs.

She reached the top step and paused on the deck before throwing back her head, squaring her shoulders and striding away from him. She took two steady steps before wavering, her face going apple-green again.

Brad scrambled after her and wrapped an arm around her waist. Oh damn. Bad idea. She felt even better close up. Like Christmas and his birthday rolled into one. "Here, grab on to the railing and stare at the horizon."

"What? Why?"

"Trust me. It works."

Her lips tightened into a line again and she clutched at her stomach, eyes closed.

"That's going to make it worse," he whispered in her ear. From their stations around the boat, the crew watched Brad and Parris's entire exchange. Well, watched Parris. Women with gorgeous legs, skimpy dresses and three-inch heels were not frequent visitors to *Tabitha's Curse*.

"I don't care if it makes it worse." Then she let out a moan that negated her statement and swung against him. She clearly wasn't going to last long if he didn't take desperate measures.

Brad moved behind her, planting his legs on either side of her, then took her hands with his and placed them on the railings, locking their fingers together. "Open your eyes."

"I don't like being told what to do."

"If you don't open your eyes and look at the horizon, I will tickle you."

That did the trick. She swung her head around to glare at him. "You wouldn't dare."

"Try me." He grinned. "Now if you're going to stare at something, look at where the water ends and the sky begins instead of at me."

"Why?"

"Oh, for God's sake, Parris. Do you have to question everything I tell you? Just do it."

Icicles would have shattered in the cold glance she gave him, but after a second, she did as she was told. He remained where he was, holding her tight.

A stupid plan because, being so close to her, in such an intimate position, had his mind on everything *but* what was in the ocean below them. He could feel every curve of her body, every breath she took. As the boat rose and fell with the slow curl of the waves, so too did his libido.

Well, that only went *up*.

Oh damn. "You, ah, feeling better now?"

"Yeah. Uh, a lot." She let out a breath and shifted forward.

Thank God. He swallowed and released her, backing away and willing his body to stop responding to hers.

Yeah, he'd have better luck telling the sun to stop shining.

"I have some…" His mind drew a blank as he searched for the name of the animal he was here to find. "Whales. Yeah, whales to look for. I should leave you alone. Look at the horizon whenever you feel ill."

But she didn't release him that easily. She turned, putting her back to the railing and her emerald eyes on him. His feet refused to go anywhere. "Why whales? What do they have to do with squid?"

"Do you know anything about giant squids?"

She grimaced. "Only that the thought of them turns my stomach."

He chuckled. "Well, I suppose they are kind of gross. But fascinating."

"See, this is why you need a makeover. Probably a dating counselor. Squid are not 'fascinating' conversation with a woman you're interested in."

"You think I'm interested in you?"

She opened her mouth. Closed it. Opened it again. "I never said that."

"Then I can talk squid all I want, right? Save the sparkling tidbits for the other women."

Once again, she looked as if she were about to say something but then thought better of it. "Then by all means, tell me about your squid and whales. Why are you so interested in squid anyway?"

"It's not really all squid. Just giant squid. They're real, but they're also mythical in a way because no one's ever seen one alive."

"Ever? Then how do you know they exist?"

"Because we find dead ones all the time. Two have

washed up in Florida, one in nineteen sixty-nine and one in nineteen seventy-eight.''

"That doesn't seem like a lot.''

"Well, those are the, ah, whole ones. A lot more are found in the stomachs of whales and parts are found in fisherman's nets.''

"Eww.'' She looked at the horizon again. "So you're out here to try to find a live one?''

He laughed. "I think every marine biologist from here to New Zealand would give his right arm for that. No, what I'm hoping to do is catch a sperm whale going after one for a little lunch and maybe get some pictures. Catching a fifty-foot squid isn't in the plan for today.''

"And how are you going to get a picture? Jump in there with your Kodak?''

"Rover's going to help me.'' He gestured toward a bright yellow waterproof video camera attached to the cabling and crane on the bow. "Jerry, my assistant, and I are going to try to get some candid shots of a sperm-whale buffet. They're the only known predators of the giant squid. If you can't find the prey—''

"Look for the hunter.''

"Exactly.''

The shared thought connected them for a moment, drawing their gazes and minds together, charging the air between them. For an instant, he wanted to draw nearer to her, to prolong the moment. How long had it been since he'd let a woman into his world?

Easy answer. Never. No woman Brad had dated had ever taken an interest in what he did, especially

Susan. Parris came from the same stock and yet she seemed different from Susan in so many ways.

But in the end, Parris lived in the world he'd escaped. The same flash-and-dash society his mother wanted him to rejoin, tie in hand. Parris was the wrong type of woman for him and the last one he should be thinking about kissing. And yet he did think about it—constantly.

What was it about this woman that simultaneously infuriated and attracted him? It was as if he saw something of himself in her, and at the same time, she brought out the worst in him.

Out of the corner of his eye, he saw a burst of water, then a long brown-gray torpedo shape gliding along the ocean surface. "Turn around," he said softly. "And look."

When she did, she gasped in surprise. "It's a whale!"

"Yep. A sperm whale to be exact. See the little hump on the back, followed by a row of bumps? It's hard to see, but his head is huge and boxy. Sperm whales have the biggest heads of all the mammals in the world. It's almost a third of the whale's whole length."

"Really?"

"Yeah. The shape of their head and the coloring tells you it's a sperm whale."

"It's so...big. I never thought..." Her voice trailed off, her jaw slack.

"The males can grow to be up to sixty feet in length. This one's not that big, maybe twenty-five feet. He's probably a teenager."

"Will it get closer to the boat?"

"Maybe. Sperm whales can be pretty friendly."

She put her hand over his on the railing, in an unconscious gesture. Her touch was warm and tender.

So unlike the Parris he thought he knew. His body reacted in all the ways he'd told it not to, craving more of her touch.

"Oh no, it's going under the water."

"He'll be back. And usually where there's one, there's more."

Beside him, Parris had stilled with anticipation. Her eyes were bright, and a smile played at her lips. Her seasickness forgotten, she stood at the edge of the deck, waiting as eagerly as a child beside a Christmas tree.

"There's another one," Brad said, pointing. "See how he's just hanging there, on the surface, not swimming? That's called logging. Because he—"

"Looks like a log?"

"Exactly." Once again, the shared thought seemed to draw them closer. Ignoring his earlier resolve to stay away, Brad closed the physical gap between them and put an arm around her waist, pointing out the characteristics of the new whale, showing her where the blowhole was, explaining how whalers calculated, by the animal's length, the time a whale could spend under water before needing a breath.

The boat was in the middle of a whale pod. On any other day, Brad would have been leaping at the Rover, hustling to get the camera into the water and take advantage of this prime opportunity.

But for once, his mind wasn't on work. It was on

the lithe woman beside him who was such an odd juxtaposition of bite and temptation.

And that was dangerous for his career—and for him. Very, very dangerous.

Chapter Four

The sun had already set by the time *Tabitha's Curse* chugged back into port, but Parris barely even noticed the hour. For the first time in ages, she'd forgotten about the auction and the responsibilities waiting for her on shore. She'd forgotten about everything except the amazing world Brad had shown her beneath the ocean.

Not to mention the other side of the man she had stereotyped as a beach bum.

She'd been wrong. About a lot of things.

"That was really incredible," she told him, when he joined her on the bow after having wrapped up his research and shut down his equipment. He and his partner Jerry had spent a lot of time, after the camera had surfaced, writing down their results and then packing all the computers, video screens, cables and cameras with the care of jewelers handling rare gems.

"I never get tired of being out here," Brad said.

The docks were only a hundred yards away. Parris closed her eyes, opened them, but the docks were still there. Maybe the engine would break down or the fog would reappear.

Anything to delay the inevitable return to reality. She'd enjoyed herself out here with Brad, more than she wanted to admit. Gigi, who'd spent a good portion of the day sleeping in the sun on the deck, came up beside her. Parris reached down and absently patted the chow's head.

Parris inhaled the salty air and, with it, a sense of relaxation. It had been a long time since she'd enjoyed anything. All the shopping trips, endless dinner parties...none of them held any appeal anymore. They seemed as empty as the deflated balloons at the end of a party.

"I guess today really showed me all the great things you can see if you learn to be patient." She laughed. "That's not one of my strong suits, in case you hadn't noticed."

Brad turned away from the railing. "I'm glad you enjoyed yourself. I thought you'd be bored, considering we didn't see any giant squid."

She smiled. "Giant squid aren't the only interesting things in the ocean."

Parris didn't want to tell him that after he'd rescued her from her seasickness, she hadn't been bored for a second. First, watching the whales, then watching as the camera was lowered into the water. After the Rover was on its undersea journey, she and Brad had gone into the cabin, where he had a laptop, TV screen and recording devices connected to the exploring camera. She'd been able to watch the Rover as it made its descent, glimpsing marine life in living color the whole way down.

But most of all, she'd watched Brad's face, the fascination in his eyes as he'd followed everything from the tiny fish darting by to the flick of a whale's tail as it brushed within kissing distance of the camera. He loved his work, that much was clear.

He had the one thing she had been seeking for herself. A passion for something that wasn't money- or reward-driven. Brad Smith was clearly a man with more depth than the oceans he plumbed.

He wasn't like anyone she'd ever met before. He was more...vivid. Stronger. She knew, after today, that being involved with him would require more from her than she'd ever given before.

That was something that alternately scared and intrigued her.

Brad turned back to the railing, hands draped across the silver pole. "My dream is to have enough funding to be able to attach a camera to the back of a sperm whale."

"Why would you want to do that?"

"With a remote camera, I can go where the whale goes and not be hindered by the weather above or the schedule of the boat. Plus, no one's ever attempted mounting a camera on a sperm whale before, though they've been successful in doing it to great white sharks." He grinned. "It's not easy to get a sixty-foot animal to cooperate when you want to stick something on its back."

"It's not easy to get a five-foot-seven woman to do what you want, either." She smirked.

He chuckled. "Ain't that the truth?" He ran a hand along the railing. "You're awfully nice today. What happened to the woman I pulled into my boat?"

"What do you mean?"

"The one who called me 'fisher boy' and had an attitude longer than the Gulf Coast?"

Heat filled her face. "I'm sorry about that."

"You're sorry?"

"Hey! I'm apologizing. Don't be difficult."

"*I'm* difficult?"

"You'll be swimming with those whales sooner than you think if you don't stop giving me a hard time." She put a hand on his back, pretending she would push him over.

The zap of electricity that traveled up her arm at the contact told her she was the one going over the edge. What had she been thinking? She had a business to run, not a romance to start.

Hadn't she learned love was a lot of smoke and mirrors anyway? It would dissipate as surely as the fog, leaving her on an old, stinky boat going right back to the place where she'd started—*Tabitha's Curse.* A metaphor for her life.

Brad took her hand in his, a smile on his face. "So, have you given any more thought to my request?"

"The makeover?"

"Yeah. You still owe me a couple favors, you know. I did rescue you from the sharks, after all."

They had reached the docks. The captain was cutting the engines, turning and reversing as needed to bring the boat in alignment with the wooden edge. "I can't. I don't have time."

"Can't? Or won't?"

"You don't understand. I—"

Brad jerked away. "I understand perfectly."

"It's just—"

"You don't want to sully the reputation of your business with a squid man makeover?"

"That's not it. This auction means a great deal to me. It's important to my business. I have to focus on that. Nothing else."

He took a step closer, his eyes connecting with hers. "You mean my mother's money is important to your business."

She blinked. "Your...your *mother?*"

Now he turned away, searching the horizon. "Victoria Catherine Smith is my mother."

"You never told me."

"I don't exactly go around touting my lineage. I'd rather wear squids on my shirts than the Smith family crest." He sounded disgusted when he said it, as if being a part of that family was akin to being shark bait.

The boat had finally stopped. A couple of crew members tied the ropes, then slid the gangplank onto the dock. The trip was over. There was no reason to stay onboard anymore.

"If you're one of *the* Smiths, why do you need me for a makeover? You could buy one anywhere. In fact, you could buy anything you wanted."

"It doesn't work that way for me."

She let out a gust and turned away. "You gave me this big story about being low on cash. Even had the look down with the torn shorts and floppy sandals." She shook her head. "But that's not who you really are."

"You don't understand, Parris."

"Oh, I understand perfectly. You don't want a *makeover*. Please, I'm not that stupid. If you were going to use me, try to be more creative next time."

He was just like all the rest of them. Tell her what she wanted to hear, while lying behind her back about who he really was.

"I thought you were someone else today," she said, cutting him off before he could respond. "But you're a lot like those whales. What you see on the surface is only a teeny bit of the truth of what's below. It seems you aren't at all what you project, *Bradford* Smith." She turned and stalked off the boat.

Or tried to. The three-inch Ralph Lauren heels refused to cooperate with the gangplank. Finally Parris ripped them off and threw them into the water, finishing her exit barefoot.

Damn that Brad Smith. Every time she was around him, he cost her a pair of shoes.

Merry smiled to herself and slipped her magic cell phone back into the pocket of her jacket. The little touch with the whale had been perfect. Everything was on the right track with Parris and Brad.

Well, except for that minor disagreement they'd had at the end of the trip. Why did Brad have to go and tell her he was related to that haughty Victoria Catherine Smith anyway? Cockles and grouse, if she could just get these couples to act the way she wanted them to, they'd fall in love a lot faster and her time as an old lady would be over before she knew it.

"What are you doing, Merry?" Her godmother, Lilith, had come up behind her, silent as a cat.

Merry forced herself not to jump and give Lilith the satisfaction of knowing she'd had the upper hand in sneakability. "Just admiring the view."

"Not working any magic, are you?"

"Me? Why, no." A little lie wasn't bad.

"How's the latest matchmaking effort going?"

"Oh, just perfect," Merry said. Another lie, but soon, she was sure, everything would work out. All Brad and Parris needed was more time together.

More of those magical moments.

"If I ever express interest in a woman again, chop me up and throw me overboard as shark bait," Brad said to Jerry the next morning.

"Oh, please. She was very nice and gorgeous. You got something against that?"

"Appearances can be deceiving," Brad said. He refused to dwell on the thought that he was repeating Parris's own words. She'd called him on the same thing, but she was wrong. He was exactly what he appeared to be.

No matter what she said.

Jerry ran a hand through his unruly thatch of red hair. "Maybe you're the one being difficult?"

Brad scowled. "Aren't you supposed to be entering the data from yesterday into our charts?"

"It can wait until later." Jerry refilled his endless coffee mug and pulled up a stool to the work desk. "You've got a hot, sexy woman who has the legs of a goddess interested in you and you're complaining. You're either mentally deranged or you've been spending too much time on the ocean. All that salt is rotting your brain."

"She's pretty but she drives me nuts."

Jerry laughed. "Those are the best kind of women. They keep you on your toes."

Brad shook his head. "She's exactly the wrong kind of woman for me."

"And why is that? You have something against the smart, pretty ones?"

"She's handling my mother's auction."

"Yeah, so?"

"So, that makes her off-limits."

Jerry let out a sigh. "I don't get you. If they ever make *Castaway, the Sequel,* I'll tell them to call you for the starring role as the island hermit."

"I'm not that bad."

"Oh yeah? Ever since you broke things off with Susan two years ago, you've been so antiwomen, I'd think you were heading for a monastery."

Brad put up his hands. "No chance of that."

"Well then I suggest you get yourself into the shower and over to the resort. I hear there's a party tonight."

"There's a party there every night. It's a resort, for God's sake."

"All the more reason to head over there before some other guy starts talking up Parris over the piña coladas."

"I'm not a guest."

"You're a Smith. You could get in just by dropping your own name."

"You know how I feel about that."

"Yeah, yeah. And sometimes being the son of a wealthy family comes in handy." Jerry toyed with his cup. "Though why you won't use that name for your research funding, I'll never know,'' he added in a low voice. ''A man with principles can be such a pain in the butt.''

It was ground they'd covered a hundred times. Jerry didn't understand the restrictions of the Smith name. Brad's inheritance from his father was tied up in conditions. Conditions that involved a corporate life, answering to a board of directors, not following his own path.

In his will, Bradford Smith, Sr. had made his wishes clear. Either his son took his place at the helm of the family business or he didn't get a dime.

The only way out of the codicil was if Brad's mother released him from his family business obligations. Which would mean she supported his marine biology dream—something she clearly didn't.

It didn't matter. Brad was a grown man. He didn't go around begging for family funds.

He'd make his own way, come hell or high water. Right now, unfortunately, it was low tide in his bank account.

Brad took in a breath and held it as if he could hold back the words he'd been putting off saying. ''Jerry, we're tapped out. That whaling trip took most of the rest of the research funds.''

''Uh-huh.'' Jerry had gone back to working at the computer, his shoulders hunched over the desk.

''What I'm saying is, I don't have any more money to pay you after this week.''

''Uh-huh.'' Jerry scanned down the log, entered a few more figures.

Brad let out a sigh. ''Jerry, you're fired.''

''Uh-huh.'' His fingers kept tapping at the keys.

Brad crossed to the computer and put a hand on the keyboard, stilling Jerry's hands. "Did you hear me?"

"Yep. You can't pay me. I'm fired. Yada, yada." Jerry pushed Brad's hand away. "Now can I get back to work?"

"I'm serious, Jerry. No money, no pay. For you or for me."

Jerry stopped typing and looked up at Brad. "I knew this was coming."

"I've always been open with you about the funding."

"So I put a little aside for a rainy day." Jerry peered past Brad, looking out the window at the setting sun and clear, slightly breezy evening outside. "Yep, looks like a stormy one to me. So, I'm staying."

"I can't let you do that."

"Then you better get to the gym and bulk up because you're going to have to drag me out of here. And I've had one too many pepperoni pizzas for you to get rid of me that easily." He went back to work.

Brad smiled and shook his head. "But what if I don't get the money from the research foundation?"

"You will. You've got some great research here. You found a new species of squid last month. Granted, it wasn't a giant squid, but it showed there are undiscovered cephalopods in the ocean. Plus, squid still have so many things to teach scientists about how their light-emitting organs work and whether the ammonium ions in their tissues can be used in practical settings." Jerry's eyes grew wide with excitement, as they always did when he started to talk about work. "That alone merits more research. You've discovered a lot here. I know you'll get the money."

Good thing Jerry sounded confident, because Brad sure as hell didn't feel confident.

And now Jerry was investing in him, too. Putting all his eggs in a basket that might have a hole in the bottom. Brad had two options—go back to being Bradford Smith and lose everything he'd worked for but gain money, or find a way to impress the hell out of the research foundation.

For that, he needed stellar research. Impeccable credentials.

And Parris Hammond.

Chapter Five

When Parris saw who was at her door, she broke into a run and nearly toppled her visitor with a grateful hug. "It's about damn time you showed up."

"Hey, what kind of greeting is that for your sister?" Jackie asked.

"You deserted me." Parris put a hand on her hip.

"I got married, Parris. I was on my honeymoon."

"Okay, you're excused." Parris grinned.

Jackie crossed into the living room of Parris's suite and flopped onto the couch. "The flight seemed so long. I already miss Steven and Suzy." Her hand lingered over the phone on the end table, as if she could connect with her new husband and daughter by touching the device. "Oh, maybe I should call them."

"You need to help me with the auction. We only have three days, you know, and everything is going down the drain...and then some."

"Like what?"

Parris sighed, took a seat on the arm of the opposite chair and opened her planner. "I sent the press release out in plenty of time, but now the media is saying they don't think they'll cover it because it's not 'newsworthy.'"

"What angle did you use?"

"Angle? I just said we were hosting an auction here."

"Easy fix. I'll fax over a letter and make a few phone calls to the media, stressing the benefits of the new aquarium and the undersea tank it will feature, giving people a rare up-close glimpse at those bio-luminescent things."

A ten-pound load floated off Parris's shoulders. Jackie was here and already things were slipping into place. "Good. That's one battle done. I took care of the other one, I think. The programs you had designed didn't come back from the printer right. They mixed up the file somehow and ended up printing them backward. Then they told me it would take three days to get it corrected, as if it was my fault they messed up. Well, you know me. I don't stand for retailer errors," Parris said, laughing.

Jackie chuckled. "That's one thing you're definitely an ace at—taking care of returns and bargain shopping. I once saw you handle an obnoxious salesperson at Bloomingdale's so well the store was ready to hand you a management position and a permanent discount on Prada."

Parris didn't want to feel disappointed by Jackie's compliment, but she did. She wanted to be known for much more than that...but what? Where had she truly proved herself thus far? She'd hoped she could be a success with the auction while Jackie was away, but nothing seemed to be going right. "That's not much of a talent, you know. You can't build a career on being able to exchange petites for smalls and making sure you're not overcharged."

"Oh yeah?" Jackie gestured at her sister. "What do you think we're doing here?"

Parris shrugged. "This is different."

"Uh-huh. Tell me what you did about the brochures then, shopping goddess." Jackie smiled at her sister, clearly more relaxed now that her trip was over. She kicked off one shoe and drew her leg up onto the sofa.

"I ran over to the mainland and got another print shop to do them overnight in exchange for an ad for their business on the back. They even took ten percent off the cost and donated it back to the aquarium fund."

Jackie blinked. "That's great, Parris. Wonderful idea."

"Idea? It was a screwup. All I did was scramble to get it fixed."

Jackie laughed. "All you did, big sister, was pull off a miracle. You can handle more of this than you think. See? This is exactly what I was talking about. Heck, you don't even need me."

Those words filled Parris with a fear she didn't want to describe. She couldn't do this, no matter how well Jackie thought she could return a pair of pumps. And she was tired of trying to prove she could. Getting a little discount on a print job didn't demonstrate any kind of business skills.

Life had been a lot easier when all she'd had to

worry about was being Parris Hammond, daughter of
Jeffrey Hammond and queen of the society party cir-
cuit. No one had expected anything of her but a stunning outfit and sparkling small talk. And now with
Jackie, the capable one, here, Parris suddenly felt in-
adequate.

"You're just saying that because you don't want
to do your share." Parris stood. "I'm sick and tired
of this whole thing. Fighting couples. Reluctant media. Picky caterers." She dropped the planner into
Jackie's lap. "You're here, so now it's your turn."

"You can't just dump this in my lap, Parris. It's
your business, too. Dad—"

"If Dad wanted us to succeed so badly with this,
he should have given us some kind of direction. He
dumped it on us, you dumped it on me. Now I'm
dumping it on you." Parris moved toward the door.
"And going for a walk."

Parris had run out of the room so fast she was still
wearing the tank and shorts she'd changed into after
returning from the whaleboat ride. Her hair, damp
from her shower, hung against her back like a cooling
curtain in the humid evening air.

In the sand, her sandals were more bother than anything so she kicked them off, carrying them in one
hand as she made her way down the path and to the
beach. She slumped onto the sand a few feet from
shore. She felt bad about the way she'd handled
things with Jackie and she vowed to apologize. She
and Jackie had just started having a real relationship
this summer and Parris didn't want to jeopardize that.
It was nice, having a sister.

They'd lived apart for most of their lives because they came from two of Jeffrey Hammond's many marriages. Their father had never been much for family. It had been easier to stay distant than to try to build a bridge. But now their father had forced them into a relationship by thrusting the business into their hands, bringing the two sisters together again. But that didn't change the fact that her father had been crazy for thinking Parris, of all people, could handle running a business. That was a choice akin to counting on Morticia Addams to decorate the White House.

She'd barely handled her own life up to this point. She hadn't been able to contain the Phipps-Stover situation. She'd messed up the public relations campaign. Then, on top of all of that, she'd missed the Kingmans today and undoubtedly screwed up that donation, too. Put it in her hands and the whole thing went to pot. "I can't do this. I can't do any of it. What was Dad thinking?"

Parris draped her arms over her knees and buried her head between them. She'd have a damned fine pity party and then worry about when—or even if—she'd return to the resort and all the problems waiting for her there.

The auction was going to be a failure. They'd finally found enough donors for the items they needed, but everything else seemed to be going wrong. Maybe Jackie would be able to resurrect it and pull everything off.

"The ocean is a lot prettier when you actually *look* at it."

Parris jerked her head up. Brad Smith stood beside her in a short-sleeved light blue shirt and tan shorts.

From this angle, his legs looked longer, his shoulders broader. For a second, she thought about burying her head against his chest and letting him carry her worries for a while.

Instead, she cleared her throat. She was Parris Hammond. And Parris Hammond didn't rely on men.

Ever. Especially not one who turned out to be the exact opposite of who she thought he was.

"I've been here for several weeks," she said. "The ocean is the same as it was when I first arrived."

"It changes every day. Every minute, in fact."

"It's water. It's blue. It comes in, it goes out. That's it."

"You've been spending too much time in malls."

She gave him a sour look. "And you've been spending too much time playing 'Bash the Debutante.'"

He lowered to his knees. "That came out wrong. What I meant is most people take nature for granted. To you, it never changes because you only see it from far away."

"In case you haven't noticed, I'm sitting on the sand." She picked up a handful and let it sift through her fingers, then waved toward the water. "The ocean is eight feet away. That's as close up as you can get."

"You can get much closer, if you want to." His gaze met hers and she knew he wasn't just talking about their proximity to salted H_2O.

He meant another kind of close. Another ebb and flow, another want and need.

She swallowed, her breath tight in her throat. She didn't want Brad to kiss her. She didn't want him to get any closer. She didn't want to trust him, to rely on him, heck, to even like him.

But she did.

Her focus went to his mouth. His lips curved into a half smile, one that she could feel reflected on her own face. Unbidden, her tongue slipped along her upper lip, as if her body was sending signals that her mind refused to acknowledge.

She didn't want—

But, oh, how she did.

"Why aren't you inside at the party?" he asked.

"I wasn't in a party mood."

"Then I have the perfect antidote." Brad put out his hand to her and she took it, forgetting what she had resolved just hours earlier, drawn by hormones that didn't care what her common sense had to say.

"Come on. I want to show you something," he said.

"I should—" Should what? There was nothing waiting for her now. She'd left Jackie with everything, at least for now. For the second time today, Parris was free of the auction. Of responsibilities. Of her schedule. She didn't have a purse, a cell phone, or a personal digital assistant with her.

There was just the golden wash of the moonlight on the sand, the quiet swish of the ocean tide. And Brad.

"Okay." She took his hand and rose with him.

"You're agreeing just like that?" He grinned. "Do I have the right girl?"

"Don't press your luck, squid boy," she said. Her voice, however, lacked its usual bite.

Had to be the moonlight. The seclusion of the

beach. The vulnerable state he'd caught her in. Nothing more.

"At least I've moved up the food chain from fisher boy to squid boy," Brad said, still holding her hand and leading her along the sand.

"You consider squids an advancement?"

"Cephalopods are quite smart. Scientists have taught octopuses to navigate mazes and remove lids from jars to get to their food. Show me a fish that can do that."

She shook her head, laughing. "Sometimes you scare me."

"You ain't seen nothing yet, baby."

The joke set her at ease and made her forget that she'd had a hell of an exit earlier. She shouldn't trust him, this man who said one thing about himself and lived another way. And yet, somehow, she did. Wasn't that who she was, too? A woman who was one thing and was working on leading another life?

He led her past where the resort property ended, past the edge of the trees, to where the beach whittled down to a narrow strip, flanked on one side by age-old palms.

"Are you taking me someplace where you can get a little revenge for when I pushed you off the dock?"

Brad laughed. "That's a damned good idea. But, no, I have something better in mind."

"Better?"

He merely smiled.

"You're probably going to tie me to a tree, drizzle me with honey and leave me for the fire ants."

"That's the best idea you've had all week."

"Torture me until I agree to that makeover you want?"

He took a step closer, taking both her hands in one of his, as if he were about to get out the rope and do just that. "Would you, if I did?"

She broke away and stepped back. "I don't know why you want my opinion anyway. I haven't exactly done the best job as a consultant for this auction. Or even for myself."

"You? You always look amazing. Like you stepped out of a catalog."

She grabbed at one of the palm trees and swung around it, the rough bark chafing her hands. "It's easy for a woman to do that. All she has to do is open up to a page or point to a mannequin and order everything on it. The model has already done all the mixing and matching."

He hooked an arm onto the trunk and looped around the tree to meet her halfway. "That's not true. You have an extra something—"

"Attitude?"

"Well, there's that." Brad grinned. "I still can't believe you used the word 'disembark' on my boat."

"A college education is a terrible thing to waste."

Brad shook his head. "Tell that to my mother. She thinks my whole degree is a waste of time." He took in a breath and she wondered about what that pause meant, what he was leaving unsaid. "Anyway. That's not a topic for tonight. Or any night, far as I'm concerned." He took Parris's hand, leading her away from the tree and over to the edge of the shore. An uneven circle of water shone against the sand, carved by the inward swishing of the tide. "Here, look at this."

"Look at what? It's a puddle."

"That's because you only see it from far away. Get up close, Parris, and see the miracles." He bent down and swished his hand in the water. When he did, a burst of yellow-green light appeared at the water's edge.

"Oh! What was that?"

"Dinoflagellates. They're single-celled algae that let off a light when they're disturbed. Some think it's a defense mechanism."

"Can I...can I try it?"

"Sure."

Parris knelt at the edge of the tide pool and dipped her hand inside, swirling it in a circle. The color flashed again, like turning on a light switch. "That's incredible. I've seen the lights along the edge of the island at night but had no idea it worked like that. I thought it was pollution."

He laughed. "No, it's as natural as you can get."

"Are you sure they aren't irradiated or something?"

"Nuclear fish?" Brad shook his head. "No. Not at all." He knelt beside her and pointed toward the water. "They're too small for me to show you with the naked eye, but under a microscope, you'll see they're just marine plankton that have two flagella, movable protein strands that work like fins and help them move through the water. They spiral more than swim, but they can move fast."

"Do they all do this?" She moved her hand again,

her eyes wide and amazed when the algae responded
with another light show. "All the time?"

"No, not all of them. Only some have biolumines-
cence. It's a chemical reaction that works with an
internal clock. They produce the greatest amount of
the internal chemical that makes them glow two hours
after nightfall."

"Which is now."

"Exactly."

"But you said it was a defense mechanism. How
does it make them less attractive to light themselves
up?"

"When they sense a predator, they flash the light
and hopefully illuminate something more appetizing
nearby."

"Get the attention onto something else."

"Right."

"The exact opposite of what women do," she
joked.

"Some women don't have to flash anything at all
to get attention," he said quietly. "They're lumines-
cent all on their own."

He could swear she colored in the darkness, but
then she turned away and dipped her hand in the water again. "Are they the only animals that do this?"

Brad cleared his throat. Stick to safe subjects, he
reminded himself. "There are lots of other marine
animals that do this. There are some squid species
that have bioluminescent capabilities, too. But they
use it for other purposes."

"Like what?"

"To attract mates." He turned toward her and she
lifted her head to look at him. "There are two species

of octopods, the *Japatella* and *Eledonella,* that have green light organs around their mouths.'' He traced a circle around her lips, slow and easy, as if drawing glow-in-the-dark symbols on them. In the moonlight, her lips seemed larger, more tempting. ''The males see them and they're goners.''

''Drawn right into the female's lair?'' Her words came out in a breath.

''Hmm.'' He didn't care about dinoflagellates or octopods or, hell, anything in the food chain right now. All he saw in the soft glow of the moon was Parris. She seemed to be lit from within, much like the creatures they'd discovered together. He looked at her mouth and knew he was a goner, too.

She didn't say a word. Her breath went in, out. A heartbeat extended between them.

And then he leaned forward and kissed her.

The flash of light in the tide pools held nothing over the brilliant burst in his head the minute his lips met Parris's. A jolt of electricity ran through him, pushing him forward. He cupped the back of her head, his fingers tangling in that blond mane.

She opened against him, her tongue teasing his, asking for more. Her arms went around his torso, holding him tight, as if she were afraid to let go and break the spell between them.

She was as sweet as dessert, tasting of cinnamon and vanilla, smelling of chocolate. Brad scooped her up and pressed her to the soft sand. His brain had stopped thinking about anything but her. He moved against her, drawing her tighter into his arms.

Parris jerked away and scrambled to her feet. ''This is crazy. I don't even want to kiss you.''

What had she been thinking? Brad Smith was the wrong man for her. Parris had decided that only this afternoon when he'd proved he was like every other man she'd ever met. He wasn't who he purported to be. He wasn't interested in her for her mind. He'd concocted this crazy makeover scheme as a way to get close to her, nothing else.

She needed to focus on her own life, on her fledgling business venture, not on him. He was a distraction. A hindrance to her goals.

A damned good-looking distraction, but still.

Her resolve had returned just in time, thank God.

Brad had drawn away from her. He rose, a tall, stone sentry in the darkness. "Sure seemed like you wanted to kiss me a second ago."

"You imagined that."

His gaze caught hers, hard and sure. "Oh yeah?"

Parris willed her heart to stop racing, her mind to stop spinning thoughts like a runaway tumbleweed. "Yeah."

"So if I kissed you again right now, you'd hate it?"

"I'd probably slap you." She could lie with the best of them. If he did kiss her again, she didn't know what she'd do. But slapping him wasn't anywhere near what her body had in mind.

"I have no doubt you would."

"Good. Long as we're straight."

"Then there's only one thing to do," he said, taking a step closer to her, coming within an inch of her mouth.

She drew in a shaky breath, her pulse screeching

within her like an Indy 500 car on a hairpin turn. Anticipating. Wanting. "What?"

His attention flicked from her eyes to her lips and then back to her eyes. He was going to kiss her again. He was going to open his mouth to hers, take her lips and do that wonderful thing all over again. And this time, she wouldn't say no, wouldn't pull away, wouldn't stop him.

Because she'd lied right through her teeth about not wanting a kiss. She wanted that one and this one and all the ones that came afterward.

"Stay the hell away from each other." His face hardened, then he turned on his heel and walked away.

Chapter Six

The minute she reached the resort property, Parris reminded herself of the several dozen reasons why kissing Brad Smith had been such an enormous mistake. She'd made him mad. Good. Now it would be easier to avoid him.

Not only had she crossed the line with the son of the woman whose auction she was organizing, but she'd also done the one thing she'd long ago vowed never to do again—

Let a man into her heart.

Men let her down. Men broke her heart.

Her father had taught her that, when he'd left her mother, who could—and often did, after a substantial investment in facial treatments—pass for Parris's twin. Garrett had done that to her, by sending her a note the day they were supposed to be married, saying he'd changed his mind because he didn't think she was the kind of woman a man could marry.

She didn't want to get married anyway. It had to be this silly resort that had her even thinking about it. All these couples, falling in love and mooning over each other like there was an epidemic of romance on Torchere Key.

Down the beach, Parris could see a wedding taking place against the picture-perfect setting sun. She walked along the sand until she reached the fringes of the circle. Merry was there, as proud and beaming as if she were the bride's mother. The wedding was a small affair, a dozen or so people in attendance, the kind of intimate, cozy gathering Parris had always dreamed of for herself.

A crazy thought. She wasn't going to get married. Men didn't look at a woman like her—a society princess—and think simple wedding on the beach and a couple kids in a two-story Cape. To be honest, she wasn't even sure she thought that about herself. And yet, sometimes, in a weak moment, she craved that very thing.

Jeez. She needed to stop getting so much fresh air. It was clearly messing with her head.

The breeze carried the words of the wedding down the beach, like romantic music. "Do you, Ruth Fernandez, take Diego Vargas to be your husband?"

Parris recognized the slim, dark-blond-haired woman now. She worked at the hotel. In her knee-length, spaghetti-strap white dress, with her hair loose about her shoulders, she looked so different.

Then Parris realized what made the difference in Ruthie today. She was happy. Ruthie took her groom's hands in her own and met his dark gaze with one so filled with love, Parris had no doubt they were marrying for the right reasons. She didn't see any vestiges of "pookie" and "sweetums" in their connection, just something real and true and based on a depth she'd never expected to find on a beach in Southwest Florida.

Around them, the guests, who appeared to be relatives of the groom, looked on with happiness. A set of parents, a set of grandparents, a sister with her two children, all dressed in pretty summer attire.

"I do," Ruthie said, and the guests beamed.

The minister asked the same question of the groom, whose eyes had never left his bride's. "I do. Forever," he said. He was dressed simply, in a white shirt and dark pants, but his tall, solid bearing spoke of the precision of a military man.

A few minutes later, the couple kissed and began their own version of happily-ever-after. Parris wished them well. Some people, she was sure, did last forever.

But not her. Not her father and mother. Parris left Ruthie and her new husband behind and headed up the beach to the resort lobby, which was quiet now that evening was well underway. She could hear a party coming from the Oasis swimming pool, but she avoided the noise and lights, opting instead to enter the hotel building and head down the hallway to the suites.

Parris paused outside her sister's room. A soft light shone under the door. She took a deep breath and knocked.

"Parris! I thought you'd packed your bags and headed for Europe." Jackie had changed into shorts and a T-shirt and had pulled her hair back from her face. She carried the file of papers from the auction, sticky notes marking pages like white flags admitting defeat.

"I'm sorry."

Jackie blinked. "You're…sorry?"

"I blew up at you and I shouldn't have."

Jackie leaned forward and peered past Parris, down the hall. "Are you sure you're the right person? Not some alien version of my sister?"

"Hey, I'm apologizing. Don't make it difficult or I'll take it back and book that flight after all."

Jackie grinned. "Now that's the Parris I know." She opened her door wider. "Come on in."

Parris entered and took a seat at the small round corner table. "Why don't we order in some room service?"

Jackie sighed. "Parris, I have no time for a pajama party. This auction—"

"And work on the auction together." Parris rose, took half the stack of papers out of her sister's hands and put them in front of herself. "We might make a better team than you think."

Jackie arched a brow.

"Have faith," Parris said. "Because I think that's the only thing that's going to make this auction come together in the next seventy-two hours."

Brad had paced his floors so often last night that even Gigi had given him a couple barks of irritation for disturbing her sleep. Try as he might, he hadn't been able to close his eyes. Every time he did, he saw Parris Hammond's emerald eyes, luminous trusting pools, drifting shut just before his lips met hers.

And his world turned upside down.

He shouldn't have kissed her. That had been mistake number one. No, his first mistake had been letting her into his boat.

Something about her had touched him, entered into that deep, dark part of him he thought he'd closed up, sealed off and welded shut.

Apparently he'd sprung a leak.

Gigi barked again, this time by the door. "All right, you do deserve a walk." He snapped on a leash, leading the chow into the bright sunshine.

His feet didn't follow the usual morning path. Gigi didn't seem interested in the trail that led through the palms and back to his tiny apartment, connected to the research building.

Yeah, right. Gigi would have followed her master to Timbuktu if he'd asked her to. It was his own two feet that took him toward the resort, around the front and over to the side where the extended-stay rooms were located. A lone towel lay on the sand, probably belonging to one of the early-morning swimmers out in the calm water.

Brad's attention returned to the buildings. Would Parris be behind one of those blowing curtains? Would she step out here, wearing nothing more than a flimsy negligee, and make all his late-night fantasies come true?

There was a movement behind the curtain of the first room and Brad paused, pretending to let Gigi sniff at the sand. A smile started to curve across his face when he saw a flash of pink silk moving forward onto the balcony.

His smile disappeared when he saw the old woman

in curlers and fuzzy rabbit slippers wearing the nightgown.

So much for *that* fantasy.

"Come on, Gigi. Time to get back to work." But his eyes lingered on the balconies.

"Let me guess. Squid on your shirt, nice dog by your side. You must be Brad," said a female voice behind him.

He pivoted and found a slim, dark-haired woman clad in a bathing suit grabbing the towel off the sand.

"How'd you know?"

"I'm Jackie, Parris's sister." She extended a hand to his. "She tried not to, but she ended up talking about you more than the auction last night."

"She did?"

"You're driving her to distraction, which, in my opinion, is a good thing."

He noticed her dark eyes twinkled with amusement. And maybe a bit of approval? He chuckled. "I'm not so sure about that. In fact, I'm not even sure she likes me." Though when they'd kissed he hadn't had a doubt in the world about Parris's feelings.

But after she'd left...

He'd had enough doubt to last him a week.

"She's a hard case, but a softie underneath." Jackie wrapped the towel around her waist and started finger-combing her hair.

"Are we talking about the same woman?"

"Oh, come on, admit it. You think she is, too."

He smiled. "She surprises me. Often. She's not always what she appears at first glance."

"That's definitely true." Jackie smiled. "You know, there's a dinner tonight for the auction donors.

Being part of the team that's putting it on, I have an extra ticket.'' She arched a brow at him. ''Do you own a suit?''

''Of course I do.'' Though whether it would fit, he had no idea. He'd never even opened the box from Brooks Brothers his mother had sent him two years ago.

''Then wear it. I'll have the ticket sent over to you later today.'' She started to walk away, then turned back. ''One more thing. Parris says she doesn't believe in fairy tales, but underneath it all, she's a sucker for a happy ending. So break out every Prince Charming trick you have.'' Jackie tossed him a grin, then made her way up the beach.

Gigi let out a bark, as if in agreement.

''You know how I feel about suits,'' he said to the dog.

Gigi barked again.

''And women in general.''

Gigi whined.

''You're right. There would be a lot of wealthy people there. The Kingmans, for instance. Some of them might even sit on the board for the research foundation. I could go for…career reasons.''

Gigi sighed and laid her head on her paws.

''And I'm only wearing a suit because it's a good professional move. *Not* to impress Parris Hammond.''

Gigi snarled.

''In fact, I won't even look her way.''

In response to that, Gigi rolled over and played dead.

Merry saw Parris enter The Banyan Room from one end and Brad enter from the other. After the way

Parris had hightailed it back to the resort the night before, Merry had been sure this was going to be her first matchmaking flop. She'd be stuck in orthopedic shoes forever.

But no, here they were, in the same room. A prime opportunity to work a little magic—*if* her godmother didn't catch her. Merry glanced over at the front door. Lissa was busy greeting people and making sure the table settings were perfect, serving as a right hand to Jackie and Parris. In other words, her attention was diverted.

So if Merry cooked up a little mood music or an "impromptu" run-in between Brad and Parris, no one would be the wiser.

She smiled to herself, then circled her finger toward the band. They segued from the upbeat tempo they'd been playing into a slower, more romantic melody.

Parris hadn't noticed, though. She was crossing the room in Merry's direction, about five feet away. Away from Brad. Merry twitched her nose and flicked her finger, first at Parris, then at Brad.

She hadn't done it fast enough. "What was that?" Parris asked, approaching Merry.

"What was what?"

"That thing you did with your finger."

"Thing I did?" Playing dumb was the best course, Merry figured. Let people think she was getting dementia. Probably the only course right now. She'd never been caught by one of the matchmakees doing her thing. How the heck was she supposed to get out of this?

"You pointed at me, then at…" Parris turned and

looked over her shoulder, in the direction of Merry's magical vibes. "Ah...at Mr. Smith."

Merry raised her hand and let the fingers tremble a little. "Merely an accident. Arthritis, you know. Makes me go all twitchy sometimes." She flung a finger up, then another out. "Oops, there it goes again."

Parris gave her a dubious look, so Merry threw in a third frantic digit movement. "You should see a doctor about that," Parris said finally.

"It's a temporary condition." She smiled. "Should be gone by the end of the summer."

Or sooner, if you hurry over to that handsome man you're supposed to fall in love with.

Parris opened her mouth to say something else, then shook her head and walked away.

Well, I'll be. Parris Hammond speechless. Maybe next I'll see pigs flying with the gulls.

Parris refused to look at him. Or even acknowledge he was there. She had a job to do. Plenty on her plate without adding Brad Smith into the mix.

Then why did she find herself pivoting to catch a glimpse of him in the dark navy suit? His tie was a jumbled mess, as if he'd never gotten the hang of a Windsor knot, and his collar looked like it had been pressed by a monkey with an iron, but overall, the effect was...

Jarring.

She hadn't expected to find Brad Smith this handsome. Or this sexy.

But he was, more than she wanted to admit. He had been, even in the shorts and tank top on the whaling boat. And in the pale blue short-sleeved shirt that seemed to glow under last night's moon.

Whoa. For a woman who didn't want to think about him, she was doing some pretty damned heavy thinking.

"Miss Hammond?" A petite woman in Donna Karan, carrying a miniature Doberman with a crystal-studded collar, came up to Parris.

"Yes, I'm Parris Hammond."

"Victoria Catherine Smith." She extended one bejeweled hand. "So pleased to finally meet you in person. I met your sister earlier. You two are both beautiful young women."

So this was Brad's mother. She couldn't have been more different from her squid-slogging marine biologist son if she'd tried. "It's a pleasure to meet you, too," Parris said, shaking hands with Mrs. Smith. The other woman's many rings cut into Parris's palm. "I'm looking forward to your auction in two more days."

"I do hope it goes well. I want the aquarium to be something really..." Victoria's voice trailed off for a second and she took a glance around the room. "Special."

"It will be. Everything's right on schedule."

No lightning bolts struck her dead in the middle of the posh Banyan Room. She was safe from the flames of liar's hell for now.

"Glad to hear it." Victoria patted Parris's hand. "Your sister Jackie tells me you're single."

"Uh...yes." Oh, no. She could already feel where this was leading.

"You should meet my son, Bradford. He's a smart

young man. Wonderful personality.'' She leaned forward, clutching the mini dog to her chest. ''A little rough around the edges looks-wise, but all he needs is a good woman.''

Clearly Parris was being sized up for more than one job tonight. ''Actually, I've met him. He's very nice.''

She could practically feel the flames licking at her feet now. Describing Brad as a ''nice'' man was an understatement to the nth degree.

''You've met him?'' Victoria's eyes took on an inquisitive look. ''And you liked him?''

''Yes, of course.''

''Well, maybe you could help me with another project,'' Victoria said, lowering her voice. She stepped closer to Parris, draping an arm over her shoulders as if drawing her into her confidence. ''Since you've been such a pro with the auction and all.''

''Well, I wouldn't say—''

''Brad needs help,'' Victoria went on, as if she hadn't heard a word Parris said. ''He's a little distracted. He's a man, you know.''

''I noticed.'' *Often.*

''My son is…determined to follow his own path. Even if that path leads him straight to the bottom of the ocean,'' Victoria said, displeasure clear in her voice. ''I'm sure, however, with the right influence, he could see his talents are best used elsewhere.''

''The influence of a woman, you mean.'' Parris didn't bother phrasing it as a question because she already knew the answer.

Victoria nodded, a hint of a smile on her fuchsia

lips. "A beautiful woman who's got his best interests at heart, of course."

"Mrs. Smith, I could never steer Brad toward anything. I mean, we hardly know each other." Parris cast a quick glance at the ceiling. Still no lightning bolts came out of the sky to strike her down in her Ferragamo heels.

"He's kept his eye on you all night. I'd say he wants to get to know you very well." Victoria smiled. "You're an intelligent woman. Surely you can see that for Bradford, using his brains in a business environment would be far smarter than spending his days in some silly rowboat looking at dead fish."

Parris thought of the day she and Brad had spent on the whaling boat, the magical night by the tide pools, of the fascination on his face every time he came eye-to-eye with an ocean creature, and felt herself bristle, but she tamped it down. Victoria Catherine Smith was her client—her only client right now.

The business was Parris's livelihood. Part of her decision to make a new life for herself, whatever that might be, with this chance her father had handed her. Despite that, she wouldn't betray a friend for it. But she also wouldn't ruin the auction. No matter what, Parris couldn't afford to tell Victoria what she really thought. "Brad, ah, doesn't seem the corporate type."

Victoria patted her hand. "That's just because he hasn't met a woman who encouraged him. He's been…drifting." Her smile widened at her pun.

Parris sent a glance Brad's way. He looked ready to die in the suit, as if the mere presence of neckwear had him feeling suffocated. She couldn't imagine him

in a suit every day, sitting behind a desk. On the
ocean, he'd seemed at home.

Happy as a clam in wet sand.

Why did he want the makeover then? Was he gear-
ing himself up for a corporate job? She couldn't
imagine it, but maybe he was.

"I don't think I'm the right woman for the job."
Parris turned toward the bar and accepted a fruit-
topped cocktail from the bartender. She'd guzzle
down arsenic if it would get her out of this thorny
situation. She looked toward Jackie, hoping for an
escape route, but her sister merely flipped her a
thumbs-up and went back to talking to the Phipps-
Stovers.

"I think you're the perfect woman." Victoria laid
a hand on Parris's shoulder, then withdrew it to stroke
the sleeping dog in her arms. "You know, I have a
number of friends involved in events such as this.
Auctions. Gallery openings. Charity dinners. I'd love
to be able to recommend you and your sister to
them."

The promise was clear in Victoria's voice. Make
Brad come around to his mother's vision and Parris
and Jackie's business could be set for the next twenty
years.

"Well, you think about it," Victoria said after a
second. "I want to go say hello to Morton Kingman."
She walked away, as if she hadn't just dropped a
loaded bomb in Parris's lap.

A bomb that involved the one man she'd promised
herself she'd stay away from not five minutes earlier.

Brad could see the trouble brewing from ten miles
away. His mother with Parris Hammond. Undoubt-

edly, she was convincing Parris—and anyone within earshot—that Brad belonged in the corporate cage, fodder for the other CEO lions.

His mother gave him a little wave, using her dog KayKay's paw. Then she went back to stroking Morton Kingman's ego, gesturing toward her son as she spoke.

Oh Lord. Now she was recruiting help from the sidelines.

He shouldn't have worn the suit. It gave his mother ideas, not to mention made him feel uncomfortable as hell. He never had mastered the tie thing. The silk crimson looked like it had been knotted by a three-year-old.

He'd burned his thumb pressing the collar and used too much starch on one side, so half of it stood stiff against his neck while the other side kept flopping inside the jacket's lapel as if trying to hide from the crowd.

He might as well face facts. He needed help. An extreme makeover for the suit-impaired.

Then he took a second look at Parris and knew damned well why he'd worn the suit.

To impress the goddess in the sea-green dress who was pretending not to notice him and doing a terrible job of it. If getting her attention meant wearing a gorilla costume, hell, hand him a banana and a fur coat.

Because that kiss had been the only thing he'd thought about for every waking minute. And every second of REM sleep.

Brad tossed back the rest of his champagne, laid the flute on the tray of a passing waiter and crossed to Parris. The closer he got, the faster his heart beat, as if it were a homing beacon acknowledging her proximity.

"You look stunning," he said, his voice low and just between them, "like a mermaid in the ocean."

She paused, her breath a hitch, then she cocked that Parris smile he'd come to know—and know to duck from. "And are you trying to net me for your evil devices, fisher boy?"

"Oh, if I could, I would. You still owe me a favor or two." He gave her a grin. "But I have a feeling you'd put up a fight."

"You've got that right." She turned, picked up a clipboard and began comparing the list on her board to the place cards that had yet to be picked up by the front door.

"And what if I did catch you? And decide to keep you?"

"For what? Some fantasy happy ending?"

"Hey, it worked out for Ariel and Prince Eric."

"That was the Disney version. The real mermaid tale didn't end with a sunset and a kiss." She finished checking names and moved over to the donations table, where a few of the items for the auction had been set out as a preview for the guests at the thank-you dinner. "The Brothers Grimm were a lot more realistic."

Brad stepped around her, so that he was now between her and the table. He noticed her attention go to the suit, her eyes light up with approval, then she washed the look away with a blink. "You know what your problem is?" he said.

"A man in a suit blocking my line of sight?"

"Besides that."

"Besides that, I have no problems." She stepped to his right.

Brad moved with her. "You live in a world of black and white. No gray, no rainbows."

She snorted. "What is this, *The Wizard of Oz?* I have news for you. Rainbows don't last."

"How do you know?"

"They disappear, Brad. You can't count on them."

"Just like you can't count on men, huh?"

"When did I say that?"

"You didn't have to. It's written all over your face every time you look at me. It was in your voice when you ran away after that kiss on the beach."

"I did not run away from you. *You* walked away from *me*." She took a step closer, her pen now directed at his chest, as if he were one more thing on her checklist. "I'd say you're the one who's scared."

"Me? I'm not scared of anything except great white sharks that haven't eaten in the last week."

"And women who might expect more out of you than you're willing to give?"

"What's that supposed to mean?"

She shrugged. "You're the one with the college degree. You figure it out. And if you can't, maybe you can ask those smart octopuses for help."

Then she turned on her heel and went back to her guests.

Brad wanted to throttle something. He'd never met a woman who infuriated him more. She was right about one thing, though—he was better off sticking to cephalopods than females.

* * *

The rest of the night, Parris noticed Brad. He was always within her peripheral vision, as if the sight of him had been burned on her retina. She saw him chatting with the guests, greeting the Phipps-Stovers like old friends, chatting with the Kingmans, talking with several of the other donors. He seemed to be everywhere.

Of course, he was in the same room as her. That did make for close proximity.

She would *not* look at him. She'd walked away with a hell of a closing line. Leave it at that and concentrate on work. That was priority one. Not the fact that he sent her head and her hormones into a raging turmoil every time he was nearby.

"Mr. Kingman," she said, putting out her hand in greeting as she approached Morton Kingman. The rotund man had on a bright purple suit with a pink shirt and floral tie. His much-younger blond wife was dressed in gold lamé, with a scoop front that redefined daring.

"Parris! What a beautiful name. And city." Morton let out a hearty laugh. "Have you ever been there?"

"No, I'm sorry to say I haven't."

"Oh, my dear, you are missing an adventure! You simply must go!" Morton pouted, lips sinking into deep jowls. "Though there isn't much marine life there. Such a pity. France really needs some whales. Maybe a few sharks. Perhaps Candy and I can start a sea-life revolution on our next trip abroad. So, tell me, what's your favorite?"

"Favorite?"

"Why, sea creature, of course. Myself, I'm partial to manatees." Morton leaned closer to her. "You are what you love, you know," he said, clutching his generous belly and laughing.

"Manatees are…nice," Parris said. What else could she say? Cute? Cuddly? Wet?

"And what do you love?" Morton put up a palm. "Wait! Let me guess." His gaze skipped over her. "Tall, statuesque blonde. Self-assured yet a tad vulnerable. You must be a fan of—"

"Mr. Kingman, really, I don't think—"

"No, don't tell me. I'm very good at this, just ask Candy. She loves silver dollars, don't you, baby?"

Candy clutched at Morton's arm and looked at him with adoration. "Oh you know me too well."

He patted her arm, right over the four-carat diamond. Parris wasn't so sure Candy was after the silver kind of dollars at all. "I do think our dear friend Parris is a sea horse lover. Independent woman, but at the same time looking for a man who is strong and dependable enough to carry half the load."

Parris let out a laugh that sounded almost hysterical to her ears. "I don't think so."

"Oh, you may not think so, darlin', but your true ocean heart never lies." Morton nodded. "Our sea selves are our honest selves."

"And my Mortie knows his stuff," Candy said. "He's a genius."

Morton smiled at Parris. "You need to find another sea horse and have yourself some ponies." He laughed at his ocean humor, then patted her hand. "I like you, Parris, and not just because your name reminds me of a beautiful city."

"Thank you, Mr. Kingman."

"Mortie, please. If I'm going to be making out a

generous check to this charity auction for the aquarium, the least you can do is call me by my first name.''

"Mortie it is, then.'' She'd swayed the Kingmans over somehow...somewhere between the manatees and sea horses. She didn't care how she'd done it, just that it had happened. Something was *finally* going right with this auction.

And that felt good. Damned good. For the first time in her life, Parris could feel success. Her own success, not someone else's. She could do this. She envisioned a career ahead of her, a path of her own making.

"That Brad Smith, he's a good guy,'' Morton continued. "Said such nice things about you that I knew I had to support this cause, even if his mother drives me up a wall.'' Morton scowled. "A dog lover, that woman. You know what they say about dog lovers?''

"Uh, no.''

"That they're fans of fur, not fins.'' He shook his head. "Doesn't matter. You have Brad Smith's endorsement. To me, that's as good as gold. Expect a check in the morning. And I'll throw in one of my rare Manatees by Mark Monetee paintings for the auction, too.''

Parris bit back her emotions enough to thank the Kingmans several times for their generosity and drew them over to Victoria's table to share the news. Then she walked away, heading straight for Brad.

"Why did you do that?'' she said when she reached him at the bar.

He thanked the bartender for his rum and Coke, then pivoted toward Parris. "Do what?''

"Put in a good word for me with the Kingmans?''

"I thought you could use the help. After all, it was partly because of me that you missed their brunch and your opportunity to convince them to donate."

"Why? You think I'm not good enough or smart enough to handle this auction? Do you think you have to keep coming to my rescue?"

"No, I just thought—"

"Listen, if I need a knight on a white horse, I'll whistle. Until then, just stay out of my business." She turned on her heel and walked away.

"Hey, Parris."

She pivoted back. "What?"

"To whistle, you just put two fingers in your mouth, you know. And I'll come running to do your bidding, princess." Then Brad gave her a teasing grin that sent her frustration level into the stratosphere.

If she'd had a magic wand right now, Parris would have turned Brad Smith into a toad.

Chapter Seven

"I take it the evening didn't go well?" Jerry asked Brad the next morning.

"What makes you say that?"

"You're torching your tie over a Bunsen burner."

"Hate the things. They don't do a damned thing for me anyway."

"And you can't tie one to save your life."

"That too." Brad tossed the charred fabric into the wastebasket. He'd thought it would make him feel better to see it disappear, but it didn't.

"So what went wrong?"

"What went right would be a better question. The only one who paid me the slightest bit of attention was Morton Kingman and that was only to get information on Parris. He threw in something about putting in a good word with the committee for me, then asked whether Parris would be attending the awards dinner with me. I might as well have been invisible."

"Well, you are a bit hard to...digest." Jerry raised an arm over his head and ducked.

Brad tossed a crumpled wad of paper across the room and conked his assistant in the elbow. "Are you saying people get sick at the sight of me?"

"You use all that scientific language when you talk to them and their eyes start to glaze over. They look like a bunch of penguins stuck inside an iceberg."

"Gee, thanks."

Jerry shrugged. "Anytime."

Last night had proved Jerry right, though. Every time Brad tried to make a case for his giant squid research to any of the aquatic donors, he'd lost them as soon as he'd uttered the word *Architeuthis*.

Clearly, changing into a suit wasn't enough. If he wanted to make a dynamic presentation, he needed to polish more than his wingtips. He wanted to be valued for his research, not his name or his connections. But unless he found a way to excite the committee about his data, he wouldn't be able to get the dollars he needed.

"Maybe my mother is right," Brad said, making sure the gas was off on the Bunsen burner before turning to the last bit of research left to do on the samples he'd collected last week. "Maybe I should go back to the corporate world."

"What, and leave all the dead algae and tentacles behind? Are you nuts? You could have this," Jerry shook a jar with a formaldehyde-preserved squid inside at Brad, "and you're thinking about a company car and health plans?"

"There are benefits to a real job, you know." Brad

loaded the slide onto the compound microscope and adjusted the magnification settings.

"Like what? A hot secretary to take 'memos' and add a little sweetness to your coffee?" Jerry scratched at his chin. "Hey, wait a minute. Why don't *we* have a secretary like that?"

"Because we can't even afford ourselves, never mind any help." Brad focused the lenses on the slide, adjusted the eyepiece to fit against his face, then studied the specimen, making little notations on a pad by his side.

"I'd gladly take a pay cut if it meant we could get a pretty—"

"Oh my God." Brad jerked back from the microscope, blinked at Jerry, then pressed his face to the eyepiece again. "It can't be."

"Evidence of merpeople? If you find a mermaid, I get first dibs on her, considering I've been dateless longer."

"No, better," Brad said. He increased the power on the lenses, then refocused.

And stared at a miracle he'd waited an entire career to find.

Parris had twelve hours to pull off the final details for the auction. Jackie had woken up with a migraine that morning and begged for a couple more hours of a dark room and peace. Parris had assured her sister she could handle everything.

She prayed she didn't prove herself a liar.

"Miss Hammond?" Lilith Peterson, the resort's concierge, was the first to greet her in the lobby. "I hate to be the one to tell you this, but the chef just notified me the menu will have to change.''

"What? Why?"

"The prime rib shipment didn't make it onto the ferry. Someone left it on the docks, where it sat all night, unrefrigerated, because it had been unplugged for loading."

Parris's grip on her planner tightened. "Let me guess. Now it's E. coli on a plate?"

"Exactly."

"What can he substitute?"

Lilith put a bright smile on her face. "Chicken."

"How original." Parris withdrew a pen and flipped to the page for the auction's menu. She doodled for a second, thinking. "We could have seafood."

"At an auction to raise money to *preserve* ocean life?"

"You're right. Might not be so nice to see a dead fish on the plate at the same time we're asking for money to support live ones." Parris tapped her pen against her lip. "Okay, I'll meet with the chef in a minute and we'll think of something. Maybe color the chicken brown and drench it in au jus sauce. Call it mystery steak." She smiled.

Lilith blanched.

"I'm kidding." Sort of.

No sooner had Lilith left than Joyce Phipps-Stover came striding down the hall, a porter struggling to keep up with her, juggling two wheeled suitcases and three handled ones. "I'm leaving, Miss Hammond."

"But the auction is tonight," Parris said, hurrying to catch up. "You'll miss the whole thing." She put

on an encouraging smile. "It's going to be a wonderful event."

"I won't be attending, nor are my husband and I
donating that stupid piece of art."

Oh no. Not another disaster. Not with only a few
hours to go. Jackie wasn't going to be the only one
reaching for the headache medicine today. Parris's
spirits plummeted.

"You're withdrawing your donation? But you
can't do that. It's the day of the auction."

"It hasn't been auctioned off yet. We certainly *can*
withdraw it. I'm leaving because that husband of
mine is an idiot and I don't want to look at his face
for one more second." Joyce snapped her fingers at
the porter. "Get me a car and get me to the airport
as fast as possible."

"B-b-but," Parris sputtered.

"There are no buts and there is no painting. I'm
sorry, Miss Hammond, but that thing has nearly cost
me my marriage. We aren't going to donate it to some
auction and give that bad luck to someone else." She
gave Parris a little nod and walked away. "I wish you
well."

The prime rib had become prime food poisoning.
The Phipps-Stovers' painting was gone. What else
could go wrong?

When she saw Merry Montrose hustling over to
her, Parris considered running away to avoid more
bad news. The resort manager hustled across the
lobby as fast as she could in her clunky senior citizen
shoes. When she reached Parris, her face looked
ashen and she had a palm pressed to the left side of
her chest. Maybe all the effort of moving so quickly

had exerted her too much. "Was that Mrs. Phipps-Stover leaving? *Without* her husband?"

Parris sighed. "Yes. And *with* her painting."

"Why didn't you stop her? Or do something?!" Merry almost shrieked the words. "Anything but let her leave without her husband!"

What was with this woman? She seemed so invested in the marital future of this couple. She was annoying, like one of those elderly neighbors who had nothing better to do than stick their noses into everyone else's love lives.

"Mrs. Phipps-Stover seemed pretty determined," Parris said. "I'm sure they'll work it all out. Any couple that calls each other 'poopsie' on a regular basis is destined to be together."

Merry inhaled, then let the breath out slowly, her hand still against her chest. Lord, was the woman going to have a heart attack right here in the lobby? Parris knew some first aid, but not enough to stop a cardiac event. And besides, she didn't have time for the resort's manager to try playing dead today.

"Yes, you're probably right," Merry said after a minute of deep breathing. "Their marriage will be okay."

The old woman was definitely one of those closet matchmakers. As long as Merry kept her two-by-two hands off Parris, they'd get along just fine.

Merry Matchmaker or not, she did a great job as resort manager and had a number of qualities that reminded Parris of a girl she'd known in college. The manager wasn't all bad, just a little too…involved for Parris's tastes. And that thing she did with her finger…

Well that was just creepy. Like a live-action *Bewitched* rerun.

"Is everything on track for the auction tonight?" Merry asked.

"Oh, sure. Just fine," Parris said, pasting a nice, big, fake smile on her face. No need to worry this hippity-hearted woman any more.

"Good." Merry smiled, too, but hers had an almost apologetic look. "Then I suppose it won't bother you too much that the florist had to run off site and *might* not be able to finish getting the decorations up."

Oh no. Not another thing. "Why?"

"His mother was rushed to the hospital with an acute attack of appendicitis. He's all upset. Went through ten hankies this morning, poor thing. His assistant is on vacation, and the other helper is attending some workshop on floral design up in Boston." Merry patted her hand. "I'm sure everything will be lovely all the same."

"Lovely is the perfect word," Parris said, sarcasm weighting her words. "Absolutely perfect, given the way everything has gone for this auction." She dropped her planner onto the lobby desk and ran a hand over her face. "I'm going outside for a second. I'll be right back."

Merry's mouth opened, closed and her hand went back to her chest. Parris could not deal with that right now. She needed a moment. Maybe a lot of moments. She spun out of the lobby and away from the mounting problems.

Once on the beach, she kicked off her heels and let her bare feet squish into the soft, dry sand. She ignored the stares of the sunbathers who clearly wondered what a woman in a bright lime Kenneth Cole suit was doing barefoot on the beach and crossed to the ocean. She dropped her matching shoes onto a dry patch of sand and waded into the water up to her ankles. The cool water hit her skin like a salve, sending a sense of calm through her.

It was so unlike the world where she'd grown up, the world she'd left to come down here to the resort and get her first taste at a career of her own. A few months ago, she'd been more worried about what time the mall opened than whether a charity would raise enough money to support its penguin exhibit. She'd spent her nights at parties, her mornings nursing headaches.

Now it all seemed like years of fluff. Like she'd been stuck in cotton candy.

She'd so wanted the auction to work out, to prove herself. But all she'd proved was that she couldn't handle it. Left under her tutelage, *everything* had gone wrong.

She let out a breath, hands on her hips, and faced the horizon, the resort at her back. She drank in the view, letting it ease her worries. After a moment, she bent down, swishing her hand in the salt water. Beneath her palm, a whole world swirled back and forth. Minnows darted along the shoreline, empty shells tumbled in the curling tide, smooth rocks peeked under the pristine sand. A ray glided across the smooth sandy bed. A tiny pale orange crab scuttled away, disturbed by her presence. Down the beach a pair of terns dodged the incoming tide.

Here, it seemed everything was perfect and real.

The problems of the auction disappeared, washing out to sea with a slim piece of sun-bleached driftwood.

"It's amazing, isn't it?"

Brad's voice. It sounded so natural behind her, as if he was part of the ocean, too. She didn't turn around, just stayed where she was, bent and staring at the wondrous world below her. "Someone told me I was looking at the ocean from too far away."

"Someone wise and intelligent. Someone very handsome, too, with a killer personality."

"Someone who often presses his luck." She stood, pivoting toward him. "What brings you to this side of the island?"

"I found something," Brad said with a smile. "Something big."

"What do you mean?"

"I need to do more tests, but I think, well, I hope…" He ran a hand through his hair, as if he'd lost his train of thought somewhere there. "Remember that day I rescued you?"

"Vividly."

"I had gone diving earlier that day, before I found you, and had taken several samples from the water. I'd found a few *Illex illecebrosus* and had come across a barracuda finishing his lunch. I'd thought it was the remains of an *Illex* because I could see tentacles, but I was wrong. Anyway, I was just getting to the last of the samples last night and in it…" His voice trailed off and he took in a breath, grabbing her hands as he did. "In it was a tissue sample from a giant squid."

"Really?" Parris's eyes widened. "Are you sure?"

"The probability is ninety-four point—"

"Brad, a yes or no would do."

He grinned. "Sorry. I'm a scientist. I'm reasonably sure. How's that?"

"About as good as I'm going to get from you, I guess." She smiled.

"You're right about that." Silence extended between them, broken only by the soft swoosh-swoosh of the ocean. The cool water swirled around Parris's ankles, tickling at her skin, reminding her that she was standing in the middle of the surf in a business suit talking to a bearded man in shorts. If she hadn't looked crazy when she'd been dabbling in the water, she sure as heck must look it now.

"I'm glad for you, Brad, I really am." She strode out of the water, back up to the beach and grabbed her shoes off the sand.

"Do you know what this means?"

"You'll finally get that research grant you need." She smiled at him and realized that no matter what Victoria Catherine Smith wanted, Parris knew Brad wanted that grant. And because she liked him, she wanted it for him, too.

"Maybe. Maybe not. I heard another scientist found evidence that bluefin tuna comingle during migration. That's a big find because it blows previous theories about them out of the water. Maybe theories about other migratory fish, too. The competition's tight."

Parris smiled. "You'll do fine."

He let out a gust and started following her up the beach path. "I don't think so. I need your help. Now."

"Now? I can't do anything right now except save

my own skin.'' She shook her head and increased her pace. "No. Sorry, Brad. I can't help you.''

"I didn't mean this second. After the auction is okay. I know that's today.''

"I'll be going back home to Manhattan then.'' Even as she said the word, though, the city didn't sound like home to her anymore. Home, oddly enough, seemed to be here.

"You're avoiding me.'' Brad grabbed her arm and gently spun her around. "Admit it.''

"I am not. I have a business to run.''

"Then tell me what your next project is.''

Fixing her own life. Finding out who she was, beyond being the daughter of Jeffrey Hammond and the sister of Jackie Hammond. And finding out what she was good at, besides mixing and matching designer outfits. "I can't tell you. That would be violating client privacy.''

"Bull. You're afraid of getting involved with me so you come up with one excuse after another to avoid me. It's simple. You owe me a favor. You refuse to repay it.'' He released her arms and took a step back. "Go ahead and run, Parris. You do it well.''

She let out an indignant gasp. "How *dare* you?''

"How dare I? How dare you? We shared something that night by the tide pools and you won't admit it. Instead, you insist on driving me completely insane. I must be a glutton for punishment because I keep coming back here, asking for more. I thought I saw something in you, but I was wrong.''

His words hit her like a punch. They were the ones

she'd been waiting to hear. All the men she'd ever dated had said them, at one time or another.

She wasn't the woman he wanted. Wasn't who he thought she was.

Parris bit her bottom lip and swallowed the lump that had formed in her throat, like a ball of candy was stuck there. "You *imagined* something in me."

He saw her as the girl on the whaling boat. The one by the tide pool. He was wrong. That wasn't Parris Hammond. Even she wasn't sure who Parris was anymore. There was no way Brad could know her better than she knew herself.

"No, I didn't." He took a step closer to her and caught her chin in his hand. "Why are you so afraid of letting down your guard? Of being who you really want to be? Just once?"

"I'm myself." Her voice sounded defensive to her ears.

"*This* is you?" He gestured toward the suit. "The woman in the power suit, barking orders, demanding perfection? Or are you the one I saw a few minutes ago, her eyes wide with wonder at the sand crab scuttling by her feet?"

She raised her chin out of his grasp. "I was relieving a little stress and cooling my ankles. Nothing more."

"Oh, get real, Parris," Brad said, letting out a chuff of frustration. "And when you do, you know where I am."

She watched him stalk off. She should let him go. After all, she had a million details to take care of today, a hundred things to do in the next hour. A dinner to plan, a pulled painting to replace, flowers to find.

Damn that Brad Smith. He'd had the last word once already with her. Once was enough with Parris. She stomped after him, her bare feet gaining little traction in the soft sand, causing her to struggle against the beach. By the time she caught up to him, her perfect chignon had come undone and her unbuttoned suit flapped against her waist. "You're not the only one with a problem or two, Mr. Smith."

He spun around, clearly surprised to see her there. "And what do you mean by that?"

"You have a family fortune you've turned your back on so you can go panhandling—"

"I'm not—"

She put up a hand. "Begging for money from a grant committee. And all because you won't tell your mother what you really want to do for a living."

"It's not that simple. If it were, I'd have done it years ago. There are complications. Strings attached."

"And you're not a man who likes strings, are you? Out there on your boat all day, calling your own shots, making your own hours. You like that life." She took a step forward, fingering his lapel, watching his eyes widen when she did. "And if you had a sexy woman who came up to you and said she wanted to tie a few strings with you, maybe one around a white picket fence and a house with a two-car garage, you'd probably run for the hills."

"Are you offering?"

"Are you accepting?"

His jaw steeled. "No."

"See, proves my point. You are not as perfect as

you'd like to think. So don't go telling me how to live my life."

She noticed she was still holding his lapel. At the same moment, he seemed to notice, too, and the silence between them stretched from milliseconds to seconds to a half minute. Their gazes connected, held, and something tightened between them, as powerful as the lure of the moon against the tide. She opened her mouth to say something, realized there wasn't a word in her head, and shut it again, breathless and mute.

"You make me crazy." Brad's voice was low and dark.

"You do the same to me." Her vocal cords strained to be heard, the words coming at a whisper.

"What do you think you're doing, walking on the beach in this suit?" He fingered the edge of her jacket, slipping the fabric between his thumb and forefinger, the bright green material sliding smooth as velvet against his skin. "You've come undone, Parris Hammond."

"I wanted to catch up to you."

"And give me a piece of your mind?"

She nodded. "Yeah."

"Anything else?"

She didn't dare respond. She wanted to shake her head no. There was nothing else she wanted to give him. This was a man who infuriated her at every turn, who seemed to have ready answers for her life, when he didn't apply a single one of them to his own.

And yet, with his hazel eyes on hers and his fingers running up and down her jacket like they were caressing her skin, she found herself unable to say a word.

They were virtually alone, caught behind some palms, shaded from the beach and blocked from the resort. The grove of trees suddenly seemed smaller, tighter, darker.

"You make me crazy," he said again, in a whisper, and leaned forward, covering her mouth with his own.

Oh, Lord. Her senses exploded.

This was what she wanted. This was what she'd come after him for. This was what her body had needed and what her mind told her to run from.

Because trusting a man, loving a man, relying on a man, led to heartache. Empty promises. Broken dreams.

Oh, how she wanted to believe Brad was the kind of man who would be different. Who wouldn't turn tail and run after it was too late—

And her heart had already been ensnared like a dolphin caught in a tuna net.

His arms went around her, sneaking under the jacket, slipping against the soft fabric of her camisole, sending music up her spine. She leaned into him, not feeling the roughness of his beard on her face anymore. She opened her lips to him, inviting his tongue in, asking him to play.

He moaned and tilted his head, nibbling along her chin, her neck. Everything inside her gut went hot and molten with desire. She reached beneath his tank top, caressing his rock-hard muscles, slipping her hands over the planes of his chest, roaming to his back and then again to his torso. His hands echoed hers, slipping up the front of her shirt. For a second, their knuckles brushed between the fabric, twin thoughts serving only to stoke the flame between them.

When he cupped her breasts, she gasped, arching against him, wanting to become putty in his hands, wanting to throw her doubts into the ocean and let them wash away.

And yet at the same time realizing how that would risk her heart if she did.

"I can't," she said, breaking away from him. "I can't."

Then she fled, taking her regrets with her.

Chapter Eight

Merry ducked behind the palm tree and pressed a hand to her heart. For the second time today, her cardiac chambers were doing the mambo. First the Phipps-Stovers, now Brad and Parris. She needed to catch her breath and stop panicking.

It wouldn't do to have a heart attack on the back lawn of the resort and be caught spying. The two of them were like a pair of Ping-Pong balls flying fast and furious from love to hate.

What was wrong with these two? Couldn't they see a fairy tale when it smacked them in the face? With the Phipps-Stovers feuding and Brad and Parris refusing to fall in love, her youthful self had never seemed so far away.

"Troubled, dear goddaughter?"

Merry stepped away from the tree and turned to face her godmother, who'd come up behind her, silent as the wind. "How do you do that? I never even heard you."

"I'm nimble." Lissa smiled.

"I used to be, too, before you cursed me. Don't you think I've learned my lesson yet?" Merry threw up her hands. "I get it! True love is wonderful. People live happily ever after. They appreciate each other, etcetera, etcetera."

Lissa's smile turned into a frown. *"Meredith."*

Merry let out a heavy sigh. "I'm sorry. I'm in a bad mood. Parris and Brad refuse to be happy together, no matter what I do."

Lissa shrugged. "Then don't do anything at all."

Merry's heart fluttered like a butterfly that had overdosed on nectar. "Are you saying let *Nature* take its course?"

"Well, it works for millions of other couples."

"No way. I don't want to be an old lady one more second than I have to. If I have to wrap these two in a magic bubble and send them off—"

Lissa tick-tocked a finger at her. "Now, Meredith, you know you can't do that."

"I'll do whatever it takes."

Lissa gave her a quick, one-armed hug. "Then get in there and help Jackie and Parris pull off an amazing auction. Relieve her stress and maybe she'll be more inclined to fall in love."

Merry scowled. "You know how I feel about Parris. I never liked her when we went to school together. Now you want me to *help* her?"

"All the more reason for you to get to know her now. See how much she's grown and changed." Lissa gave her a gentle shove in the direction of the resort. "It will do you both some good."

Merry harrumphed. "All I need is for Parris and

Brad to stop fighting the happy ending I'm bound and determined to make them have.''

Merry marched off across the sand. Well, marched as well as one could in support hose and orthopedic shoes.

The auction was in full swing by the time Brad arrived, this time wearing the second suit his mother had sent him, since he'd torched the tie that went with the first one. He'd done an equally bad job of botching the neckwear the second time around and gave up when he realized he was already twenty minutes late.

His mother had, as promised, sent over a ticket for him to sit beside her at the head table. He wasn't going to go until he'd seen the program booklet she'd included and read the last-minute changes printed on a sheet inserted into the fancy paper. One little addition to the auctioned items list—a replacement for the contentious Phipps-Stover painting—caught his eye and sent him scrambling for the second confining Brooks Brothers suit. He'd called Jerry, run his plan by him, gotten an enthusiastic shout of support, then struggled into the suit.

"Bradford! You came!" His mother rose from her seat and clasped both his hands.

Brad kissed his mother on the cheek, catching the scent of Chanel No. 5 as he did, then sat as she retook her chair. "You did send a ticket."

"You can represent the family interests then, darling. I'll add you to—"

He put up a hand to stop her before she had him in a corner office with a prime parking space. "Mother, I'm here because I'm your son and because

I'm a marine biologist. I'm supporting the aquarium because it's going to be a place where people can learn about aquatic life.''

"Oh." His mother gestured toward a table of suited men. All of them had gray hair, as if years of working behind a desk had taken a toll. ''But don't you want to meet the members of the Smith Company board? They all flew down for my event. There's John Becker, the CEO of—''

"No, Mother. I don't." He clasped his mother's hand. "I'm here to see you and bid on something at the auction.''

"You're going to bid?" She arched a brow. "With what?''

"I have money." The last of his grant, and every penny he could cobble together, with Jerry's blessing.

"From what?" She let out a laugh. "You don't earn money catching dead fish for a living, dear.''

"That's not what I do, Mother. If you'd just—''

"Hush now. The auction's about to start." She motioned to him and swiveled her attention toward the podium at the center of the stage.

The auctioneer, a rotund man with a booming voice, stood there in a tux, holding up a Jackson Pollock painting. But Brad didn't notice the effusion of colors and lines the artist was renowned for, nor did he hear the frenzied bidding that began the minute the auctioneer announced the starting bid.

All he saw was the woman standing against the wall on the far side of The Banyan Room, wearing a long pink sparkly dress, her hair swept up into a loose chignon, tiny ringlets tickling against her neck.

Parris.

His stomach did a flip-flop, as if a team of acrobats had invaded his intestines. He pushed his plate away, food untouched. His mind drifted away again, going to Parris. To the fluid way she moved across the room, talking with guests, taking care of details as she chatted with a busboy and made sure a mess got cleaned up. She straightened a floral arrangement, tucking a stray sprig of hibiscus behind her ear as she did.

Oh God. Now she looked as pretty as the most picturesque spot on the island, more delicate than the frozen fruit concoctions the waiters were dispensing. He wanted to tear out of his seat and race down there, take that flower from her hair and trail it down her long, tempting neck, along every valley of her body, until the pale petals merged with the pastel of her dress and he was lost in the scent and feel of Parris.

Damn his hormones. He should hang them for treason.

The auctioneer brought up a guitar autographed by some celebrity, but Brad's eyes remained on Parris, now laughing at something one of the guests had said to her. "She's beautiful," his mother said in his ear, "isn't she?"

"Who?"

"Parris Hammond. She's been a wonder to work with, her and her sister."

"That's because she's smart. And organized."

His mother turned to face him, a half smile on her face. "You like her, don't you?"

Brad tore his attention away from Parris. With reluctance. "Where is this going?"

She shrugged. "Nowhere."

"Did you talk to Parris about bringing me back into the company fold?"

Victoria toyed with her fork. "I might have mentioned it."

"Did you pressure her, like you do everyone else? Promise her great things for her business, if she did what you asked?"

She swirled a bite of chicken in the marsala sauce but didn't eat it. "I told her I know a great deal of influential people. They all like to use consultants for their events. That's all. Just networking, darling, everyone does it."

"Not that kind of networking, they don't." Brad scowled and turned away.

Although his mother's interference annoyed him, he now saw Parris with renewed eyes.

He'd be damned. Parris had been offered the business of a lifetime. All she'd had to do was push him into the family business. And she'd clearly not done it. If anything, Parris had stayed as far away from trying to make him into a corporate type as she could. She'd refused to help him get made over into a suit-and-tie guy, leaving him to flounder with the damnable Windsor knot on his own.

He'd be willing to bet every dime in his pocket it was because she liked him. Jackie had been right. Parris *was* a softie.

"Why are you smiling?" Victoria asked.

"She didn't do it, Mother. She didn't do what you asked."

"And how is that good?"

"That's the best damned thing I've ever heard,"

Brad said, tossing his napkin to the table and rising.
"I think I've just upped my opening bid."

"Going once. Going twice. Sold to number twenty-
eight for seven thousand dollars." The auctioneer
gestured toward Morton Kingman and then at a six-
foot-high porcelain dolphin sculpture. "Thank you,
sir."

"No, thank you. That's going to look wonderful
beside my glass manatee in the dining room." Mortie
beamed and clasped Candy's hand.

Parris smiled. The auction was going well. The bids
were coming in just a little higher than expected and
the guests seemed to be enjoying themselves, with a
little good-natured ribbing peppered in among the
more competitive bids.

Two of the guests, Jane and Richard Worth, came
up to her. "Wonderful auction," Richard said. His
blue eyes sparkled with the delight of outbidding another competitor. "That vase I bought will look nice
in the entryway of my company. It's almost as beautiful as my wife." He gave Jane a one-armed hug.

"Then you should have bought the vase for me,"
Jane said with a tease in her eyes. "But I'm sure I'll
see something else I like before the end of the night."

"She's going to help me empty my checkbook tonight," Richard said, laughing.

"That's what we're hoping for," Parris joked back.
The duo returned to their seats, already discussing the
next items up for bid. Parris was happy to see the
guests so happy. From across the room, Victoria
Catherine Smith gave her a triumphant smile. Good.
The client was pleased, too.

Brad had left his seat at the head table. She'd seen him there, beside his mother, a few minutes earlier. He'd been wearing a second suit—dark gray this time—but not looking much more comfortable than the first time. His collar hadn't won the battle against the iron and his tie— Well, the tie looked like it was trying to commit hari-kari.

And yet, there was still something about him that drew her eye again and again, like a lighthouse. She caught him looking at her as he left the table, his hazel gaze connecting with hers across the room.

The vast, softly lit Banyan Room seemed to shrink in half. Her heart began to race and her lungs forgot to breathe. Was this what it would always be like when she looked at him?

Always?

What kind of thought was that? She did not want, did not need, did not have room for the word "always" in her vocabulary. And she'd never met a man who spoke it—and meant it—anyway.

Brad was focused on his career. On finding the elusive, ugly-as-sin giant squid in the bottom of the ocean. He'd made it clear he didn't want anything more from her than wardrobe advice. And well, a few kisses.

Okay, a lot of kisses.

Very nice kisses.

Very hot kisses.

Kisses that made her want to—

So he made her heart beat a little faster. Big deal. A good roller coaster could do the same thing and do a lot less damage in the end.

Jackie came into the room, dressed in a red chiffon

dress and clutching her handbag with two white-knuckled hands. "How's it going?"

"You should be in bed," Parris said, keeping her voice low, and moving them out of the brighter lights of the room and into the quieter area by the plants.

"I've been there all day and still don't feel well." Her sister pressed a hand to her left temple. "Boy, when that headache hit, it hit like a semi without any brakes."

"Go back to bed. I can handle this. Really."

"I should be here. Helping with—" Jackie waved her hand vaguely "—whatever needs doing."

Parris turned her toward the hall. "Go. Don't worry about anything. This is the easy part."

Jackie gave her a weak smile. "You're a good sister."

"I don't think you've ever said that before."

"Well, I better start, because now I owe you at least a dozen favors. You pulled it off, Parris," Jackie said, surveying the room. "You really did."

"No, *we* did. I couldn't have done it without you, sis."

"We make a great team." Jackie smiled. "Glad to have you as a partner."

Yet when Parris looked at the room, she saw a hundred details she could have perfected, another twenty things she could have done to make the auction that much better. But in her sister's eyes, it was good. For a second, she allowed herself to enjoy the feeling. Parris felt the beginnings of hope that this could be a viable career.

Jackie swiped a glass of water from a passing waiter's tray, taking a long sip. "Where did all these flowers come from? I thought the florist couldn't complete the order.''

"I picked them myself on the island today. I thought they'd give it a bit more atmosphere.''

Jackie smiled, clearly pleased with the choice. "It works. Really well.''

"Thanks. You'll never believe who helped me. That Merry, the resort manager. Though she did complain the whole time about how the heat was aggravating her. I swear, she reminds me of someone I used to know.''

"And probably didn't like," Jackie said with a laugh.

Parris chuckled, too. "Most likely.''

"And how are things with Brad?''

The one subject Parris didn't want to discuss. Brad wasn't as easy to deal with as a few missing flowers and a spoiled prime rib. "Shouldn't you be back in bed?''

"Not until you tell me why you're over here and he's all the way over there by the hors d'oeuvres table, looking good enough to eat in that suit. Well, except for the beard and the tie…that is a tie, isn't it?''

"Brad has neckwear issues.''

"I'd say so." Jackie grinned. "Still, why aren't you with him?''

"I have an auction to run.''

"Seems to me it's running itself. Or so my older and wiser sister told me." Jackie laid a hand on her sister's arm. "I think you're more afraid of Brad being another Garrett Brickwater than anything else.''

Parris bit back her surprise at Jackie mentioning

Garrett's name. He'd been a sore subject between the sisters, a moment in Parris's past that didn't exactly fill her with pride. After Garrett had dumped Jackie in favor of Parris, the sisters hadn't spoken to each other for years. Back then, Parris had been too self-centered to send him packing, too in love with what she thought Garrett was offering her to consider the long-term damage to her relationship with her only sibling.

When Garrett had left Parris outside the church minutes before their wedding, Jackie had taken the high road, never saying a word in retribution. In the two years since, neither sister had ever mentioned his name.

Until now.

"I was stupid when I was with him," Parris said. "I made a lot of mistakes."

"It's in the past." The gentle tone in Jackie's voice told Parris her sister meant it. Maybe the two of them were on the path toward a real relationship. Maybe they'd both grown up over these past few weeks.

"I think you're a little gun-shy," Jackie said.

Parris started to protest, then stopped. "Well, maybe a little. How many men do we know who have stuck around through the hard parts? Dad didn't. Garrett didn't—"

"Steven did."

"Okay, one happy ending."

Jackie clasped Parris's hand with her own. "If you're looking for guarantees, you should invest in a Maytag repairman."

Parris laughed.

"I'm serious. Happy endings are possible. For me and for you."

Parris looked at Jackie's eyes, shining with a joy brighter than the new ring that graced her left hand. She'd heard the love in Jackie's voice when she spoke of Steven and their daughter. It was something she'd never felt in her own life. "I envy you," Parris said.

"Envy me?" Jackie laughed. "That's a switch. Why?"

"Because *you* have it all."

Jackie blinked. "I thought you weren't into that home-and-hearth kind of thing. You were always the party girl."

"I was. But not anymore. Even parties get stale." Parris looked across the room, seeking Brad. "I want more now."

"The mortgage and the minivan?"

Parris laughed. "I don't know if I'd go that far."

"Well I would. You deserve to be happy."

She sighed. "It doesn't matter. Men don't look at a woman like me and see things like white picket fences and teddy-bear wallpaper borders."

"Maybe you're just looking at the wrong kind of men."

Parris swung back toward Jackie. "What do you mean?"

"Stop looking for the princes and look for frogs instead." She smiled. "Princes aren't much good for taking out the garbage on Tuesday nights."

"What if it doesn't last, even with the frog?"

Jackie sighed and laid a hand on her older sister's arm. "Love is about taking chances, Parris."

"I don't gamble, Jackie. Not with my heart. Not anymore."

"And next up on the auction block is a last-minute substitution," called the auctioneer. "Something a little unique."

Her cue. Parris left Jackie and crossed to the stage, stepping up the few stairs to stand by the podium. All eyes in the room swiveled toward her. So this was how a Holstein felt at a farmer's market.

"This lovely lady, Ms. Parris Hammond, has agreed to donate one week of her consulting time to the highest bidder. This time can be used for party planning—like this wonderful event—or another such important event. It's a generous offer, worth a princely sum. Who'll start us off?"

"Four hundred dollars," Morton Kingman said, raising his number twenty-eight card high and giving Parris a smile.

"Five hundred," a male voice countered from somewhere in the back, raising a number seventy bidding card. The voice sounded familiar, but with the buzz of talking people and without a face, Parris wasn't so sure who was speaking. She raised on her toes to see whose hand held the sign, then heard Mortie beat the price.

"Six hundred," Mortie said.

"Eight hundred."

Mortie scowled. "Nine hundred."

"One thousand dollars."

Parris strained higher but still couldn't see the identity of the man holding number seventy. A woman with a large, plumed hat blocked her view. The chatter grew, undoubtedly people getting a kick out of a human on the auction block.

"One thousand, two hundred dollars," Mortie said.

"One thousand, five hundred eighty-seven dollars and, hold on—" there was the sound of rattling change "—ninety-three cents and...one stick of Juicy Fruit."

Mortie threw up his hands in defeat, laughing. Candy gave him a hug of consolation for losing.

"Going once," the auctioneer said. "Going twice." He glanced around the room, now stone silent. "Sold! To number seventy for ah, a nice sum and a stick of gum."

The auction sign moved to the right, along with the person holding it. Parris opened her mouth, closed it. Blinked twice, hoping this was a nightmare.

No. It couldn't be.

Parris Hammond had just been sold to Brad Smith for fifteen hundred bucks and change. And one, hopefully unchewed, stick of gum.

She'd been wrong. Even cows were auctioned off with more dignity than that.

He'd won her, fair and square. When he saw her face across the room, though, Brad wasn't so sure Parris was going to play fair and honor her end of the bargain. He paid the cashier, got his signed receipt for one week of Parris's services, then went to find her. He had very little time to waste.

And, by the looks of his tie tonight, a hell of a lot to accomplish.

He crossed to Parris and caught his breath when he got close to her. From across the room, she'd been beautiful. But up close, she was enough to send his heart plummeting off a very steep cliff.

The pink dress scooped in the front, allowing him a peek at her delectable chest. A dab of pink gloss highlighted her lips, making it seem like they begged to be kissed. She'd sprinkled some kind of shimmer on her shoulders and neckline, so everything about her glowed.

What would it be like to taste that shimmer? To run his mouth along the hollow of her throat and down the valleys that called to him beneath that dress?

What would it be like to have her in his arms, happy to see him and not fighting him at every turn? To hear her say his name with desire, not—

What the hell was he thinking? Getting involved with Parris Hammond should be the last thing on his list. She'd made it clear he wasn't her type. Plus, he had a giant squid's existence to prove and the only reason he was here was to redeem his purchase.

A business transaction, that's all.

But when he came closer, the rest of his body considered another kind of business altogether. After he'd redeemed his favor from her, then he'd settle the unfinished business they'd started in the palm trees and by the tide pools. Parris Hammond had gotten under his skin and he wasn't going to be able to think straight until he became immune to her.

As a scientist, he knew the best way to build up an immunity was to expose himself to her. Over and over again.

Uh-huh. That should work.

It seemed to work wonders on her end, he noticed.

She had her hands on her hips and was giving him a good scowl. "I thought I made it clear I didn't think we should get involved," she said.

"I don't want to date you," he interrupted. Well, okay, he did, but not right this second. So he wasn't entirely lying. Really.

"You…you don't?" For a second, he thought he read hurt in her eyes, but then the look passed and she went back to being fire and ice.

"No. We have business to conduct." He held up the receipt.

"The certificate is good for a year." She turned away.

"I don't have a year, Parris. I don't even have a month. I paid for your services and you owe me that. Now. This week. On this island."

She wheeled around. "You're asking the impossible."

"Why? Am I that bad? That hopeless?"

"No." Within that one word, her voice had softened, become almost a whisper. He felt a twinge of hope that maybe there was something between himself and Parris and he hadn't been crazy at all. "It's not you at all. It's—"

And then another man came bounding toward them, scooped Parris up and kissed her before Brad knew what hit him. "Parris! Darling! I'm so glad to see you!"

Chapter Nine

Of all the men Parris least expected to see on the island, her father topped the list. She should have known he'd fly in at some point to check on the satisfaction of the first client in the business he'd handed to her and Jackie. He wasn't the type to make purely familial calls, never had been, no matter how often either of the girls had clamored for his attention.

Jeffrey Hammond, as he'd told his daughters often, was in business to make money. And every minute he wasn't in business was a minute he wasn't making money.

Still, a little part of her—some silly part left over from when she was ten years old, she supposed—felt happy to see him.

Parris stepped back from Jeffrey Hammond's fierce embrace. "Dad! What are you doing here?"

"Visiting my little girls and seeing how they're doing with the project I gave them." He took a look around the room at the energetic bidding and nodded approvingly. "Seems you've done well with this."

"I couldn't have done it without Jackie. She was great," Parris said. Although she'd been dragged, reluctantly at first, into this business, Parris had to admit she was proud of it now. She could look around the room and see evidence of her and Jackie's achievements. That felt good. Really good. She knew now what Brad meant when he talked about being able to measure results. She could measure this, see it, hold it.

She turned toward him now and gestured between Brad and her father. "Dad, I want you to meet someone. This is Brad Smith. He's a marine biologist who works off the coast of Florida. He has a research station on the island. Brad, this is my father, Jeffrey Hammond."

The two men shook. "Marine biologist, huh? What do you research?"

"Giant squid."

Jeffrey let out a hearty laugh. "You're kidding, right? There's no such thing as giant squid, is there?"

"Actually there are. A couple of them have washed up on the shores of Florida."

"You don't say?" her father said. "Well, that's all right, I guess, long as you don't have designs on my daughter." He chuckled. "I can just see me explaining that to the guys at the country club. 'Parris married a squid stalker.'" He elbowed Brad in the side, as if he should laugh at the joke, too.

"Dad, I've seen Brad's research. I've even been out on the boats with him. It's great stuff. You'd be impressed."

"Takes a lot to impress me." Jeffrey gave him an appraising glance. "But if you can do that, well, I'll listen."

Brad grinned. "Too bad you're not on the grant committee I have to talk to next week. I could use every bit of help I could get there."

"Grant committee?"

"The National Aquatic Research Foundation."

Her father scratched his chin. "You know, I think Larry Hudson has some pull in those circles. He could give you a hell of an endorsement. You want, I'll call him. As a favor to my little girl. Anything for a friend of hers."

Her father was at it again. Dispensing gifts with abandon. Buying love. Buying allegiance. Soon as he did, he'd be gone, figuring he'd done his fatherly duty. It was how he'd treated his daughters and his wives. Buy a trinket, then leave and move on to the next "project."

She wouldn't blame Brad for accepting. He needed the funding and her father was practically handing it to him in a gift bag. She looked at Brad, half expecting him to put out his hand and shake her father's, sealing the deal.

But he didn't.

"Thank you, sir, but that's not necessary," Brad said. "I'd rather earn the money on the merits of my research."

"Or lose it on your own," Jeffrey said. "I say a man who doesn't take advantage of an offer like that is a fool."

"All due respect, Mr. Hammond, but I have to live

with myself and I prefer to know I've done my own homework.''

Parris could have kissed Brad at that moment. For sticking to his principles, for refusing to be swayed by her father's wealth and power. For choosing the hard road rather than easy street. How many men had she met that would do something like that?

None.

Until now.

Her father considered Brad for a long moment. As the seconds ticked by, Parris waited for a blowup, the inevitable confrontation. No one ever defied her father. He'd fired people for doing less.

"I like you," her father said finally. "You have moxie. I don't meet many men like that. You ever think of leaving squids for the nine-to-five world, you give me a call." He reached into his breast pocket, withdrew a business card and slipped it into Brad's hand.

"I appreciate the offer, Mr. Hammond, but I'm not exactly a suit-and-tie kind of guy."

He glanced at Brad's mangled neckwear. "Yeah, I thought so."

"Oh, look, Jackie came back," Parris said, motioning toward her sister, who stood in the archway, a smile on her face and a much clearer look in her eyes. "She had a headache earlier but must be feeling better."

"Jackie!" their father boomed, pivoting and heading for his other daughter.

"I'm sorry about that," Parris said when her father had left. "My father can be—''

"I come from the same kind of family." Brad grinned. "No apologies necessary."

Behind them, the auctioneer was announcing a break from the bidding for a little dancing. The band picked up and started playing "Always."

"I believe that's our hint," Brad said.

"Hint? For what?"

Brad took her hand and led her toward the floor before she could protest. "For us to dance."

"I'm supposed to—"

"Be dancing with me. The auction will survive without you for five minutes."

He was so tempting. A complete distraction. Every time she was with him, she came closer to trusting him, to believing in the possibility of the fairy tale. "Is this part of your plan to convince me your make-over can't wait?"

"Can you, for five minutes, just be you and me? A man and a woman dancing together simply because they want to, not because they have ulterior motives?" He wrapped one arm around her waist and put the other hand into hers. It felt warm. Comfortable. As if it was meant to be there. "Just us, Parris. Nothing else."

She couldn't say no. She didn't *want* to say no. For five minutes, to be only him and her. No auction, no family members. Nothing but them and the sweet harmony of the music flowing between their bodies.

He pressed her torso to his. Heat lit up her skin, electrifying her nerve endings. "Lean into me," he whispered. "Dance with me."

She struggled against his request. Giving up control, even on the dance floor, meant trusting him. Brad kept his hand against her back and swayed with her, his movements soft and fluid, asking nothing more than she wanted to give.

She took a half step forward, another, then leaned her head forward a little at a time, fitting it into the crook of his shoulder.

He smelled of the ocean, like a man who worked for a living, not one who spent his days behind a desk with manicured nails and a cold heart. He was warm and alive and—

There.

So very much there. She forgot about being in charge and shifted with his movements. Her body read the cues of his, sensing his movements in perfect timing. She moved her lips closer to his neck, inhaling him, swept up in the music and the movement and everything that was Brad.

"Parris," he whispered, turning his face toward hers. His hand drifted down her back a little, accommodating the new position. His mouth was inches away, his breath warm on her lips, as if they were breathing the same air.

She surged forward and covered his mouth with her own. He tasted of promises, of hot nights spent tangled in sheets and each other. Her tongue danced with his, along and under. She tangled her fingers in his hair, wanting more. Wanting it all.

Too soon, he pulled back, an inch, maybe two. "Oh God, Parris, you're amazing."

"I try my best," she said, her voice a whisper, but the tease gone.

"We bring out the worst in each other," he said,

then trailed a finger along her chin, "Or maybe the best."

She nodded. "We probably shouldn't be together."

"All it does is lead to trouble."

She watched his lips move and thought of nothing but tasting them again. "Yeah, trouble."

"Then I'll see you tomorrow?" Brad said, smiling, clearly not caring a whit about trouble. "On the beach?"

"For what?" Her brain had become a jumble filled with nothing but him and the music, still sweeping through them.

"For my first lesson."

She shook her head. "I don't have anything to teach you."

The music had come to an end, the band pausing before switching to an upbeat tempo.

Brad skipped a finger along her lower lip "Oh, I disagree, Parris. I disagree very much."

She wasn't coming. Brad knew it. For half an hour he'd stood here, waiting on the resort's beach for Parris. He'd been a fool for thinking she'd show up.

Their kiss last night had been a dream. A fantasy. He might as well be searching for mermaids. He'd have better luck with those mythical creatures than he would with Parris Hammond.

"Looking for someone?"

He pivoted and found her behind him, coming out of the ocean in a bikini so tiny it should have been filed under some kind of indecency law.

But hell, who was he to complain about a little

scrap of crimson material? It did, after all, cover her curves. Well, the important ones.

"I didn't expect you to be in the ocean," he said when he finally found his voice.

"And I didn't expect you to be so early." She wrapped her arms around her waist, which only served to thrust out her breasts. Oh, Lord. He was in trouble now.

Growing trouble.

"Sorry. I was anxious to, ah," he said, working like hell to keep his gaze above her neckline, "get started. So why are you out here?"

"I needed a swim. I had to burn off a few…frustrations."

"From anyone or anything in particular?"

"Yeah. There's this really annoying marine biologist I know," she said, cocking a smile. "I can't get rid of him."

"Like a bad itch, huh?"

"Worse."

"Well, we'll have to see what we can do about that."

She paused, as if she were going to say something else, then changed her mind. Instead, she took in a breath and he saw her entire demeanor shift from playful to business. She bent over, giving his heart a jolt, and picked up a towel he hadn't noticed before. She wrapped it around her torso, blocking his view.

Damn.

"Shall we get to work?"

"Work?" he parroted. His gaze was still on the length of pink-and-white terry cloth.

"On your makeover. Not my body."

"Oh, yeah. That."

"Let's start here, since you've provided me with such great material already." She took a step forward and fingered his T-shirt. "Wearing a shirt that says Octopuses Make Great Bridge Partners won't endear you to anyone."

He glanced down at the shirt, bought at a convention five years ago. "Why not?"

"It's too cutesy."

"You think I'm cute?"

She let out a gust of air. "I didn't say that."

"You think my shirts are cute?"

Parris threw up her hands. "This is not going to work. *We* are not going to work. You frustrate me more than anyone I know."

"Funny, I find myself saying the same thing about you. Often."

"Then why are we doing this?"

"Because I bought you fair and square."

She muttered something under her breath that was neither ladylike nor complimentary of marine biologists with a penchant for tacky tees.

He took a step forward, purposely invading her space. "And because you need me, too."

Her gaze flew to his. "I do not."

"You are one lost woman, Parris Hammond."

She pointed at him, her green eyes ablaze with indignation. "I know exactly where I am. La Torchere Resort in Florida. I can point it out on a map and give an approximation of latitude and longitude, even if my hair color implies otherwise about my intelligence level."

"Whoa, call off the verbal Rottweilers. I never said you were dumb."

She ran a hand through her hair, displacing the wet strands. "Sorry. Most people assume—"

"Most people are wrong."

She colored but didn't say a word.

"You are a smart woman. You know the word 'disembark,'" he said, teasing.

"Will you quit it with that?"

"Never. I'll be teasing you about that until we're old and gray and sitting in our rockers on the front porch."

Where had that sentence come from? That implied permanence. Marriage, for God's sake.

Two weeks ago, that would have been the furthest thing from his mind. Brad Smith had always been a man who called his own shots. Made his own hours. Answered to no one but himself and his research logs. But now, looking at Parris, mouth agape, her eyes wide with shock at what he'd just said, he thought he'd just try the word on for size.

Marriage.

Didn't sound as much like a yoke and chains as he'd thought.

Parris blinked at him, as if she had to process the words, too. "Now, with the shorts, I think you're pretty much okay, though you might want to think about something more fitted," she went on, as if he'd never said a word.

"More fitted," he repeated, having no idea what the hell she meant.

"As for shoes…"

But she'd lost him. He heard words like "wingtip"

and "loafers" and "flat front versus pleated" and his mind wandered. To the way her lips curved when she talked. To how she focused entirely on him. She could have clothed him in a tutu and moon boots and he wouldn't have cared, as long as she kept giving him the full force of her attention.

"Is that okay, Brad?"

"Huh? What?"

"Men," she muttered. "Do you want to take the ferry to the mainland tomorrow and go shopping together?"

"Shopping?" he squeaked. No other word in the English language struck fear in a man's heart like that one.

"It'll be painless, I promise. I'll be there to help you."

"In the dressing room, too?"

She shook her head, a smile on her lips. "You are incorrigible. No wonder you get along so well with fish."

Shopping with Parris sounded…not bad. Until he remembered one painful detail. "I, ah, don't exactly have a budget for clothes. I used up my research budget for something else I needed pretty badly." He didn't tell Parris it was her.

"You are *Bradford* Smith, right? Of *the* Smiths?"

"Yeah."

"Well then, for once in your life, put that name to use."

He shook his head. "No, out of the question."

She grabbed his arm. "You want the research money, right?"

"Yes, of course."

"You're not going to get it by wearing a Squids Are Great shirt. This thing you're going to is black tie, right?"

"Yeah."

"And do you own a tux?"

"No. And proud to say it." He grinned.

She muttered another very unladylike word. "You're going to drive me to drink."

"Martinis with me, on the beach, anytime."

She sighed, as if she'd considered then rejected the idea. "Just this once, let your money help you with your goals. It's not a sin. You earned it."

"I didn't."

"You grew up in the family. You supported your mother with her dream. You were at the auction and you even bid on one of the items." She swept a hand over her frame. "You've earned a tux at least."

He considered her for a minute. "Did you ever consider going into law?"

"Me? No." She laughed.

"You'd have made a hell of an attorney." Brad shook his head, knowing he'd been beaten by a good argument. "All right. I'll break in the family credit card at the men's clothing store on the mainland. I'm warning you, though, I'm doing this at my own peril. Soon as my mother gets word I'm buying dress clothes, she'll think I'm coming back into the family fold and send me a desk set and a secretary."

Parris smiled. "If she does, keep the desk set."

"But not the secretary?"

"No, not her. Not unless she's old and ugly."

"My, my, Parris Hammond. Are you saying you might be jealous?"

She pressed a hand to her chest. "I'm not saying anything that might incriminate me."

Chapter Ten

Merry took in a deep breath. Maybe there was hope for these two after all. On her magic cell phone, she flipped through a review of yesterday's beach meeting between Brad and Parris. It seemed to have gone okay. And they had a shopping trip on the agenda today. If there was anything Merry knew Parris was good at, it was shopping.

But wait, what was this? She saw the image of something that portended bad news, then the cell phone went dead. Merry shook it, cursed at it, but it refused to return to the living wireless world.

"A pox on everything cellular," she muttered. Whatever she'd seen, it meant trouble was on the horizon for today's trip. Someone was going to ruin things for Parris and Brad.

Merry looked at her To Do list. Could she slip away, sneak onto the ferry? Tag along and intervene if need be?

There was no way this couple was going to undo all her hard work. Not after she'd spent an entire afternoon picking flowers all over the dang island with Parris. She'd needed an extra Epsom salts soak for her poor feet after that one.

She tried the phone again. No luck. Some days she wondered if she'd be better off with a Ouija board and a Magic 8-Ball.

"You're looking...neater this morning," Jerry said when he came in a little after seven.

Brad looked down at the golf shirt and dark navy shorts. A Christmas gift from his mother he'd found unopened in the back of his closet late last night, after digging past all the T-shirts, worn, frayed-cuff shorts and battered sneakers. He shrugged. "It's nothing."

"Bull." Jerry took a step closer. "Did you trim your beard, too?"

"I tried to." Brad rubbed a hand over his chin. "It didn't go too well, considering I haven't touched the thing in ages. Maybe I should shave the whole thing off."

"Let Bigfoot go?" Jerry gasped. "You've had that fur on your face ever since I met you in college."

"I'm getting older."

"All the more reason to cover your wrinkled face." Jerry gave him a jab.

"Ha-ha." Brad peered at his wavery reflection in the stainless-steel countertop. "You think women prefer a clean-shaven man?"

Jerry grinned. "You mean a certain woman named Parris?"

"How do you know about Parris?"

"I met her on *Tabitha's Curse,* remember? I have eyes. And ears. Plus, your mother stopped by the lab yesterday afternoon, when you were out gathering more samples, to sing Parris's praises as a potential mate for you. Good gene pool, apparently." Jerry laughed.

"My mother came by?"

Jerry shrugged. "Think she was spying for the competition? Or maybe just interested in what you do?"

"Knowing my mother, the former is more likely."

Jerry refilled the coffeepot and set it to brew. "You know, you're not even a half-full guy. You're more like the damned glass might as well be empty."

"Thanks, Jer. Always count on you to cheer me up."

As usual, Jerry ignored him and went right on doing a thorough analysis of Brad. "Though I have to say you have seemed more…chipper lately. And not only about the squid sample you found."

"The sunshine. It makes me happy." Brad gestured out the window.

"Yeah, sure, Kathie Lee," Jerry said. "So when do you see her today?"

Brad grinned. He never could get anything past Jerry, who'd become his best friend in the two years they'd worked together. "I meet her at the ferry in an hour. I wanted to get a little time in at the microscope first, then head over there."

"Already set up." Jerry waved at the scope. Prepared slides were stacked and labeled beside it, with one already loaded onto the base. "I figured you'd be at it early."

"The DNA tests completed yet on the first sample?" Brad didn't want to get his hopes up, not until he had scientific confirmation of a giant squid.

"Nope. Another couple days." Jerry put up a hand to ward off Brad's next question. "Before the meeting with the committee, I promise."

"I owe you one."

"Actually, you owe me a million. But I'll work for details instead of peanuts. Since I'm not dating anyone, I gotta live vicariously through you. So tell me about Parris and you. And don't leave out the good stuff or I'll send your best squid down the river."

"There's nothing to tell. We aren't dating. She's just helping me get my act together before I meet with the committee."

Jerry let out a sigh. "Yeah, right. You like the woman—I can see it in your sort-of pressed collar." His assistant flipped at the edge of Brad's shirt. "You never try that hard for me or Gigi."

Gigi let out a bark of agreement.

"Commitment isn't a bad thing, Brad," Jerry continued.

"Says you who isn't even committed to a pet."

"Hey, I said it wasn't a bad thing for you." Jerry winked. "I'm a hopeless case."

Brad shook his head. "I'm not good at it."

"You are, too. One bad engagement doesn't make for a track record of broken hearts."

"I've been with a woman like her before. Our worlds don't mesh. Sure, it's good whenever we're at the resort where everything's sort of...magic and away from the real world, but when she gets back to her regular life and I get back to mine, it'll all be over. These kind of things aren't made for anything permanent.''

"You mean *you're* not." Jerry shook his head and let out a sigh while he poured himself a new mug of java. "You can make anything work if you want it to. Stop offering up excuses and take action."

"When did you get to be Dr. Phil?"

"When I switched from decaf to regular." Jerry hoisted his cup. "Seriously, you're happier when you're with her. I say that's enough of a reason to take a chance. Live a little. Outside of the damned laboratory."

"The probability of it working out is—"

Jerry cursed under his breath. "Brad, stop being a damned scientist for five minutes and be a regular guy. To hell with the statistics. Stop thinking with your brain." He took a gulp of coffee, then put the mug back on the counter. "All it does is get you in trouble anyway."

Parris left Jackie and her father eating breakfast together. She could see the tension, built up over years of a staccato relationship, sitting between them at the table like an unwelcome guest. She hoped they were both still on the island when she returned. In her dreams, she pictured them all together someday, like one big happy family.

Another one of those stupid fairy tales that only happened in books. Just like happy-ever-after marriages and men who kept their promises.

Jackie had found her fairy tale, but Jackie was different. She hadn't grown up with the same life as Parris had, in a house filled with an endless stream of toys, her every wish indulged by an absentee father and a mother who thought things replaced love. All it had taught her was that happiness was transient. As soon as the wrapping paper was off, the feeling was gone, tucked into the trash with the spent ribbons and torn tape.

In a few days, she'd be going back to Manhattan and Brad would be staying here with his squids and his octopus T-shirts. Connecting her heart to his was a foolish mistake. Eventually the wrapping would be gone and she'd be left wishing she could put it back the way it had been.

She'd arrived at the ferry early, this time in sensible low-heeled sandals and a Nicole Miller dress. As the minutes ticked by, she began to reconsider. Spending a day with Brad would only intensify her attraction to him.

Heck, intensify? It was already at a white-hot level.

But then she saw him walking down the pier toward her. He strode with purpose, tall and strong, his tan dark against the light golf shirt.

Something within her sprang to life. A different kind of want than she'd ever experienced before. Something deep and visceral, as if leaving him would mean leaving a part of herself behind on Torchere Key.

Crazy thoughts. The sun was getting to her. Maybe she needed a higher SPF. Or maybe she needed more Brad.

"Good morning," she said, her voice light, airy, unaffected. She hoped.

"It is a good morning. Clear, not a hint of fog.

That was an odd fog we had the other day, wasn't it?''

"So thick it made me get on the wrong boat."

"Was it the wrong boat?" Brad asked. "Seems everything worked out in the end. The Kingmans still made their donation and you got to see something amazing up close."

"Are you talking about you? Or the whale?"

"The whale, of course." He grinned. "I brought you something." He withdrew a slim piece of glass from a small white box.

"What's this?"

"A dinoflagellate on a slide."

Parris laughed. "Most men bring flowers. Only you would bring a research sample."

"You'll never forget me, though, will you?"

Lord, no, she never would. She'd never be the same, either. Meeting Brad Smith had changed something within her, as if that fall into the water had been a baptism into a new life.

A new Parris.

She held the glass up to the light. She could make out the shape of the algae, including one of the "fins" he'd talked about the other night. Seeing it rocketed her mind back to that moment. To that kiss. To everything that had happened in the quiet grove by the tide pools. Parris cleared her throat. "So what do I do with it?"

"Look at it under a microscope. Then you can really see one up close." His index finger hovered over the image under the glass. "You'll never be far away again."

"But I don't own a microscope."

"Hmm. Pity. Good thing you know someone who does."

"The boat's getting underway. We should, ah, talk about the plan for today." Parris dropped her gaze to the papers in her hands.

Brad noticed she held the clipboard between them like a weapon. He could see she was going to try like hell to keep this outing all business. Well, fine. As long as he got his makeover.

Yeah, right. All he was here for was a suit. And jellyfish were merely pretty *scyphozoas* floating in the water with no ulterior motives or poison lurking in their tentacles.

"I have a schedule all drawn up," she said, producing a set of sheets and handing them to him. "I thought we'd hit the biggest men's stores first and then have a quick bite to eat before heading over to the hair salon."

Brad scanned the top paper. "Hair salon? Who said anything about cutting my hair?"

"You could use a...trim," Parris said, her tone the kind she'd use on a nervous three-year-old about to enter the barber's for the first time.

He knew, from his daily glance in the mirror, that he was more than a little challenged when it came to his hair. "What kind of cut are you thinking exactly?"

Parris took a step closer to him. She lifted a hand and touched his scalp. A thousand nerve endings ignited with her touch. "A little off here, some more off the sides. If you trim it up, you'll show the definition of your face and let your eyes..." Her voice trailed off.

His gaze had cemented with hers. "My eyes what?"

A heartbeat passed between them. Two. People bustled to and fro on the ferry, but neither he nor Parris seemed to notice. Torchere Key was filled with newlyweds, after all, and they could have been just another couple. "Your eyes are gorgeous," she said finally. "Like the ocean, only deeper. You really don't even need a makeover. You're already smart and funny and interesting." She bit her lip, as if she'd said too much.

Something within Brad softened. The hard edges on his heart wore away, the walls breaking down. Parris had done what no one else had ever done before.

She hadn't merely commented on his eyes and touched his hair. She'd looked inside him. Past other people's expectations and accepted him. She had no interest in making him into something he wasn't.

Clearly the woman he'd found flailing around in the ocean wasn't the same one standing beside him today, her eyes riveted with his. "If that's so, it's because you've stolen my heart, Miss Hammond," he said, his voice teasing, but his words no longer a joke.

She dropped her attention back to that damnable clipboard. "When the ferry docks in a few minutes, we'll have to hurry when we get off because we have a lot—"

"Did you hear what I said?" He tugged her chin upward. "I'm telling you I'm interested in you. For more than a makeover. For something that lasts a lot longer than a haircut and a new suit."

"I...I don't know what to say to that."

"Say what women normally say."

"Which is?"

"Okay." He smiled. The fear still shone in her eyes. She was afraid of being hurt, that he knew, but there was something else, something he couldn't put his finger on. "Then I'll ask you to dinner and we'll take it from there."

"No." She shook her head, stepped back a pace. "I know how it'll go. We'll go out, we'll have a wonderful time—"

"Nothing wrong with that."

"And maybe you'll even think you've fallen in love with me. Maybe I'll think the same. We'll date a while, make plans for a future. Then you'll come to your senses."

"Come to my senses?" Brad chuckled. "That's what I'm doing right now."

She shook her head. "Men like you, men in general, don't marry a woman like me. Not for the typical reasons. I'm the trophy wife. The kind you dress up and take to cocktail parties. I'm not the kind you picture feeding babies at two in the morning and driving the kids to soccer games."

"And is that their fault? Or yours?"

She crossed to the front of the boat, following behind a group of passengers getting off. He slipped in behind her. For a few minutes, neither of them said anything as they left the boat, went down the pier and into Locumbia, up to the row of shops that greeted tourists with open doors and colorful merchandise.

"What did you mean by that?" Parris said finally. "How can that be my fault?"

"Maybe you give off non-soccer-mom vibes."

"I am who I am, Brad. I don't try to be anything else." She pushed on a handle and entered the first store.

Beside her, Brad arched a brow.

"What?"

"Maybe you're the one who's afraid. Afraid of the soccer games and the two-in-the-morning feedings. And so you don't send out those vibes. In fact, you don't send out any vibes at all. Every time I get close to you, you run."

Still doing a good job of avoiding his eyes, Parris crossed to a rack of tuxedo jackets. "You know, it doesn't matter. I don't believe in all that anyway."

"All what?"

"That happily-ever-after stuff. It doesn't happen to anyone."

"Anyone? Or just you?"

She picked up a black jacket and pressed it to his chest. "I think this style would be the best for you. Tails, of course, would be out of the question. More for a wedding than a meeting. But this rounded lapel cut is a little more modern and—"

He lowered the hanger. "Parris."

She swallowed and swiveled away. "Of course, the right shirt will make all the difference. I think collarless would be nice. Maybe even a wing collar with a Euro Tie. That would be different. Help you stand out in the crowd."

"Don't ignore me, Parris."

But she did, crossing to a row of shirts and choosing the first white one she saw. "This would be great under that jacket," she prattled on, "with some cuff links, and—"

He spun her toward him. "Parris, what I'm trying to say quite clumsily is that I'm falling in love with you."

The hangers in her hands clattered to the floor. Her emerald eyes were wide, shimmering in the overhead lights. "You don't mean that."

"I don't lie, Parris."

"You barely know me."

"I've spent more time with you in the past few days than I have with anyone else I know, except Jerry. And he's not my type." Brad grinned.

Parris yanked the shirt and tux off the floor, pressed them in his hands and pointed toward the dressing room. "You'd better try this on."

"Parris—"

"Brad, we made a deal. I'm just keeping up my end of the bargain. You don't need to butter me up anymore." Then she turned away and started a conversation with a salesman before Brad could convince her otherwise.

Damn. He didn't just need a style makeover. He needed the Dating Police to help him before he messed up this relationship even more.

As soon as the dressing room door shut behind Brad, Parris allowed herself to breathe. Had he just said he was in love with her? The thought rocketed through her, coupled with hope and doubt, intertwining around the words like determined spiders weaving alternating webs.

She meandered around the shop, touching the silver racks, her mind moving faster than her feet. She'd heard those same words once before, from Garrett.

And he hadn't meant them when it came down to the moment of truth.

Could Brad be different?

She glanced toward the closed door. He was the wrong kind of man. He made her question things, question herself.

He required her to give. To think. To become more than she was. More than she'd ever been before. Could she do that?

And could she take the risk that he'd meant the words he said?

She had to say something when he came out of that room. She couldn't go on ignoring his statement. The store only had so many clothes she could throw at him before she actually had to prepare a response.

I think I'm falling in love with you.

With Parris the debutante? Or Parris who'd looked at sand crabs and glow-in-the-dark algae with him under a dreamy, starlit sky?

Dreams. That's all they were, she reminded herself. Dreams were not grounded in reality. If there was anything Parris was good at, it was dealing with the here and now. And in the here and now they were on a resort island that seemed infested with some kind of romance bug. It would pass, when she returned to the mainland and Brad returned to his senses.

Then why did her heart feel like a cinder block?

Her cell phone chirped. She fished it out of her handbag and flipped it open. "Parris, get to the mainland hospital now," Jackie shouted. "Dad's been flown over there with chest pains."

Parris was gone. Brad came out of the dressing room, expecting to see her, but found the store empty except for an eager salesman ready to help him break in his charge account.

She'd left. If it hadn't been clear before that she didn't reciprocate his feelings, it sure as hell was now.

"Sir?" One of the salesmen approached him. "The lady told me to tell you she was sorry, but she had to go. You were in the very last dressing room or she would have gone in there herself to give you the message."

"I'll bet." Brad scowled. Then he caught himself and apologized. "Thanks for the message." Such as it was.

"She seemed quite worried, sir. Even tried to charge into the dressing room herself, but we don't allow that sort of thing in here. Perhaps something happened?"

"Yeah, something did." He'd made a huge mistake, that's what.

"Do you like the tuxedo? It does look quite nice on you." The salesman motioned toward the mirror.

Brad pivoted and looked at his reflection. He hated to admit it, but Parris Hammond had been right about one thing. She knew what looked good on him. Too bad she wasn't as good about what was best for his heart.

"Will you quit fussing over me? I'm not worth all this worry," Jeffrey Hammond said. "You girls need to get back to the island and work on your tans or something."

Parris perched on the edge of his bed. "Dad, I'm not going anywhere until I'm sure you're okay."

"I'm fine, baby. It was a touch of angina and a lot of heartburn. Probably had too much Tabasco on my eggs."

Jackie chuckled. "You and your spicy foods. I told you they'd get you in trouble."

"Now when have I ever worried about what kind of trouble I'd get into?" Against the stark white of the bed linens, her father looked older, grayer. Parris realized how little time their odd family had ever spent together. Too many years had been spent in bitter recriminations.

She didn't want it to be that way any longer. She'd enjoyed working with Jackie, even though the first few weeks had been bumpy. They may not have been a huge success with their business, but they'd found a way to work together and developed a friendship. It was a start.

"You always were trouble," Parris said, smiling as she took her father's hand. "You were a bad influence on us."

"I was, wasn't I?" Jeffrey's smile turned to a sober line. "I didn't mean to be, you know. I'm just not good at permanence."

Out of the corner of her eye, Parris saw Jackie bite back a response. The divorces hadn't gone well for either of their mothers. As much as each of them loved their father, they'd both readily admit he had all the marital commitment of a guppy.

"If I were you girls, I'd think marriage was a terrible thing," her father went on. "I'd probably think most men are like me. Run out on you when you least expect it, moving on to something younger and blonder."

"Dad, we—" Jackie started.

"No, don't sugarcoat it. I'm getting old here. Had a near-death experience over my scrambled eggs. Don't interrupt me. I may take it all back when the morphine wears off." He smiled. "You know what makes men run?"

"Hormones?" Parris joked.

"Fear. Well, maybe a bit of hormones, too. But mostly they're afraid they aren't good enough for the women they picked. Both your mothers—" he reached for Jackie's hand on the opposite side and gave it a squeeze "—were good women. I didn't deserve them and they certainly didn't ask for what I gave them. Inside this big old body is the heart of a mouse."

"You? I always thought you were a lion. My father, who could take on the world."

"In business, you better not mess with me. But in here—" he released her hand to pat his chest "—I'm the biggest wimp this side of the Mississippi, especially when it comes to commitment."

"How come you're saying all this now?" Jackie asked, taking a seat on the opposite side. "Why not years ago, when we needed to hear it?"

Jeffrey swallowed. "You know why I gave you girls that business?"

They shook their heads.

"I was in the courthouse one day, signing the papers for my fourth divorce and realized I was alone again. I went back to my empty apartment and my empty life and well, hell, I felt sorry for myself." He grabbed Parris's hand again. "You two were the only good things that came out of any of my marriages.

My ex-wives all hate me, and rightly so, but to you girls, I've always been Dad, even if I was only there on holidays and birthdays.''

Parris put her palm atop their joined hands. "We're family. For better or worse."

Jeffrey's blue eyes misted a little. "Yeah, we are. And that's what I wanted more of. So I tried to get it, with the only thing I knew. A business."

"You kind of threw us to the sharks, Dad," Jackie said. "We didn't know what we were doing at first."

"But you pulled it off. You girls were amazing. I was so proud. I told everyone those were my daughters."

Across the bed, Parris met Jackie's eyes and the sisters shared a grin. They'd done it, despite the last-minute problems. The auction, Jackie had told her earlier, had raised twenty thousand dollars more than they'd hoped.

"What I'm trying to say is that you two are all I have. I don't want to lose that. And I don't want you and your sister to lose each other, either."

Parris smiled, her vision clouded by tears. "You're saying we're stuck together, huh?"

"Like it or not."

Jackie smiled. "I can live with that. Parris isn't *so* bad."

"Hey!" Parris gave her sister a light jab. "This is a tender moment here."

Jackie rubbed at her arm, feigning pain. "Not any-more, it isn't." Then she laughed, and the sound of her happiness was echoed twice over.

Chapter Eleven

When Brad got back to the mainland late that day, he'd managed to complete everything on Parris's schedule. He'd even seen the stylist who'd fussed over every hair on his head as if it was a work of art. For a man who spent two seconds a day on his hair, it had been a weird experience.

One he hoped he didn't have to repeat anytime soon.

The charge card was well broken in and he had a tux, shoes and two new pairs of pants and non-tie-requiring shirts in the garment bag over his shoulder when he stepped off the boat. Parris had made notes on his copy of the schedule about outfits she wanted to see him in, even attaching a few photos from magazines, which had made shopping on his own easier.

He hadn't enjoyed the experience, but it hadn't been as painful as he'd expected either.

He scanned the shoreline as the ferry approached

the dock for the resort. She wasn't there. She hadn't been in any of the stores, hadn't been at the hair salon, had never returned to meet up with him.

He'd screwed up. Scared her off. That falling-in-love statement had been the equivalent of dropping an outboard motor at full speed into tranquil waters. It wreaked absolute havoc and scared off every living creature within hearing distance.

After disembarking, he hesitated at the end of the dock. Go back to his apartment and start working on his presentation or…

Head up to the resort, find Parris and try to yank that motor out of muddied waters. She owed him an explanation for running out on him, especially after he'd suffered through a hair mask.

The lobby was busy, filled with auction attendees checking out and new guests checking in, creating a flurry in the forest-green-and-cream space. "Mr. Smith! I almost didn't recognize you, what with the new haircut and without your beard." Morton Kingman crossed to him and extended his hand.

"Nice to see you again," Brad said, shaking the other man's large hand. He nearly had to shield his eyes from the bright turquoise-and-lime-green suit Mortie wore today. Clearly Parris wasn't doing his shopping for him. "Are you checking out?"

"Heading to Europe for a bit. Before that summer heat gets to me." He released Brad's hand and gave him a clap on the shoulder. "You know, I've been thinking about my offer to put in a good word with the committee for you. And I wanted to withdraw it."

"Withdraw?" Brad blinked. "I wasn't intending to

take you up on it, but I'm curious about why you changed your mind."

"I know you have your ethics and all that," Mortie said. "I respect that about you. But, I also know how these committees work. They want flashy stuff they can parade in front of the alumni. Now I happen to think your work is fascinating. I've been doing a little reading on the *Architeuthis* myself."

"You have?"

"Yep. I think it's one of the greatest animals that ever lived. Not one of the prettiest," Mortie laughed, "but a pretty incredible one. You find any evidence of them?"

"Well, I don't want to get my hopes up because the DNA results won't be back for a day or two, but—"

"Yes?" Mortie's eyes were as wide as a child's on Christmas morning.

"Well, I think I found a tissue sample from one when I was diving last week."

"That's incredible! They do exist here after all." Mortie shook his head. "Amazing. What I'd give to go out and see you do your thing someday."

"I'm afraid it's not very exciting, Mr. Kingman. A lot of sitting around and waiting for luck to find us or for the camera to find a miracle."

"I disagree. And so does Miss Hammond. She said watching the Rover in the sea was exciting. She mentioned you wanted to do something with cameras on sperm whales."

Brad shrugged. "That's my dream. But for that you need funding. Lots of it. And there are lots of scientists competing for the same dollars."

"That's very true." Mortie tapped a finger on his chin, assessing Brad. "But none of them are competing for my dollars."

"Your dollars? What do you mean?"

"I'd like to be your benefactor. On one condition. You take me out sometime, let me see that camera in action. I've always wanted to get closer to the sea. And you get right in there. Hands, feet, everything."

"Sir, that's a very generous offer. Too generous. I couldn't—"

"Oh yes, you could. Just say yes. I have a foundation. I'll make it a grant, renewable each year, if you keep finding great things. Make you work for your money." Mortie winked. "How's that sound?"

"Wonderful!" Brad bit back the excitement, the ideas churning inside him. "But...don't you want me to show you my research with a formal presentation and paper first?"

"Nope. I talked to Parris Hammond at the auction. Saw her face light up when she told me about that whaleboat ride. She said she fell in love with the ocean that day." Mortie smiled. "I suspect she fell in love with more than that."

A funny feeling twisted through Brad. Hope. Maybe Parris hadn't run out because she didn't return his feelings. Maybe there had been some other reason. And maybe there was a future for them.

"Besides, you don't need to put on a suit to convince me you're smart and on to something. The report would be nice—it'll keep the foundation's board in touch with what I'm doing. Throw one in the mail when you get a chance." Mortie clapped him on the shoulder again. "In the meantime, go catch one of those giant squids. *And* the little sea filly talking to your mother over there.''

''Sir, I can't thank you enough.''

''You don't need to. You feed my fascination with the sea. That's enough. Humor me once in a while and talk my ear off about what you do.''

Brad grinned. ''It'll be my pleasure.''

''You're quite the young man, you know that? Bet your mother is proud as all hell of you.''

Brad shifted the bag on his shoulder. ''I'm not exactly doing the career she'd have chosen for me.''

''Ah, she'll come around. You gotta understand, she's a dog person.'' With that, Mortie nodded and walked away, tossing a ''good luck'' over his shoulder as he did.

Brad circled around to the front desk. He paused when he heard Parris's voice coming from a few feet away. He pivoted and saw her past the clump of foliage in the lobby, talking with his mother, as Mortie had said. He started toward her, then stopped when he caught a snippet of their conversation.

''I'm thrilled the auction went so well, Miss Hammond,'' his mother was saying. ''But now I'm more interested in the other project I spoke with you about.''

''Other project?'' Parris asked.

''My son. I heard from Ms. Montrose that you and my son went shopping today for his wardrobe. Might I assume these are business clothes?''

''I helped him, yes, but not for what you think.''

''I really want you to…encourage him to rethink his career choices. You and I both know he's smarter than this fish thing he does.''

"Brad is happy with his work."

"But I'm not. If you can bring him around, I'll make it worth your while."

Brad saw Parris straighten her spine. Her cheeks flushed crimson. "Mrs. Smith, I'm sure you're making a generous offer and I'd be crazy to turn it down considering my business is new and struggling. But I learned something today—in fact, I learned something from your son. Doing what you love and being with the people you care about is more important than money."

Victoria snorted. "That's a fairy tale."

"I used to think it was. But it isn't. You raised all this money to build an aquarium and you're never going to appreciate it. You know why? Because you've never seen any of these animals up close. I have. I've watched a sperm whale come up to our boat and flick his tail at the camera. I've held a sand crab, swished my hand in a school of minnows, seen the sea light up at night with magical algae. Because of Brad. Because of that 'fish thing' you despise and he loves."

"You should be careful what you say, my dear. Your business could be hurt by a word from me. I travel in the same circles you cater to." Victoria lowered her head, her dog close to her chest. "But if you wanted to help me—"

"Some prices are too high to pay," Parris said. "I wish you well with your aquarium." Then she left, leaving Victoria Catherine Smith openmouthed and speechless.

Brad waited until his mother had recovered her composure, then crossed to her. Her eyes widened with surprise and the knowledge that he had clearly heard everything. He gestured to her to come outside. They walked through the doors and down the lawn.

"What you overheard—"

"Was enough, Mother. I'm not coming into the family business. Ever. I'm happy here. I enjoy my research. My life. I'm doing something good, whether you believe it or not." He took a breath and tamped down his anger. He knew why his mother had done this, why she pushed so hard. "You can't replace Dad with me. It's time to move on, Mother."

"I'm not—" Her head dropped to KayKay, who snuggled against her.

"You are. He's been gone for three years. He'd want you to move on. Sell the business. Don't hang on to it for my sake."

"Sell it?" She gasped.

"Yeah. Have your own life. It's liberating."

His mother shook her head. "Bradford, I only want what's best for you."

He put out his arm and his mother took it, following along as they crossed to the beach, trailing down the path that led to the water's edge. "I know you do, Mother, but your best isn't my best."

"And I've gone about it all wrong, haven't I?"

"You try to force people into things. The more you push, the more they pull away."

She released his arm and crossed to the lapping tide. She was silent for a long time, considering his words. Finally she pivoted toward him, a shimmer in her eyes. "Did I lose you?"

"No, not at all." He took three steps forward and drew her into a hug that included the dog. A long-overdue embrace that made him realize how much he'd missed his mother in the years during their stand-off.

His mother held tight for a long time, then drew back. "I probably ruined things for you with Parris, didn't I?"

"We'll work it out. I'm the one who needs to do some romancing."

His mother stroked KayKay's head. Then she inhaled and let the air out slowly, as if reaching a decision. "Do you know why I wanted to build this aquarium, Brad? And why on this island?"

"So you could check up on me and push me into the business?"

"No...well, a little. But there was more to it than that. I raised the money for the aquarium instead of a dog shelter or an art museum or anything else because I wanted something that would—" she released KayKay to the ground "—connect me to you."

"Connect us?"

"You and I are very different, it's a wonder we're related," she said softly. "And I thought maybe this would give us something to talk about."

A smile curved on Brad's face. "It will indeed." Then he took his mother's hand and led her closer to the water. "Now, for just a minute, Mother, let me show you my world."

And when she bent down beside him, Brad knew there was hope. Even for them.

Chapter Twelve

Parris had looked for Brad ever since the run-in with his mother, shortly after her return to the island. She stopped by the lab, but Jerry hadn't seen him. Gigi had greeted her like an old friend, giving Parris the same playful nudges she dispensed to everyone else. Apparently Parris was now welcome to ride shotgun on the Zodiac.

By the time the last ferry docked, she'd given up hope. She returned to her room, regret heavy on her shoulders. She should have tried harder to talk to him before running to the hospital. The way it looked—

She didn't want to think about how it looked, because it wasn't good.

"Parris! There you are!"

She spun around. Jackie hurried down the hall toward her, clutching a paper. "This came for you, but they delivered it to my room by accident." She thrust it into her sister's hands.

Parris unfolded the single sheet. "An invitation? To a romantic evening? On the island, by the…" She smiled. "Tide pools." She looked up at her sister. "Brad."

"Well, I don't think it's the busboy." Jackie winked.

"I—I—I have to go. I have to get ready."

"Why? You look great as you are. That suit is—"

"All wrong." Parris hurried away, the paper tight in her fingers. "It's all wrong, but I can make it right."

Gigi lolled in the corner of the picnic area Brad had set up. She waited much more patiently than her owner, who had reset the champagne glasses and floral arrangement three times, aiming for the perfect tableau on the plaid blanket he'd spread out.

"Hi."

Brad wheeled around. Parris was framed by the palm trees, smiling at him. The simple curve of her lips sent a surge of joy through him.

"You came," he said.

"I'm sorry I left without talking to you. I should have told you where I was going. My father was in the emergency room. I just ran out of there. I didn't think."

"Is your dad okay?"

She nodded. "He had an angina attack. Plus, too much Tabasco gave him a little heartburn. But yes, he'll be okay." She took a step forward, her green eyes never leaving his. "But I'm more worried about us. Are we okay?"

"We? Since when is there a 'we'?"

"Since you pulled me out of the water." She took his hand in hers and raised their clasped palms to her chest.

"And into my heart."

"I did all that. On the first day?"

He chuckled. "Maybe not that first day."

She moved closer, raising her free hand to touch his face. "You look so different without the beard. And with the haircut."

"Better?" His face felt odd. Younger, lighter. More him, in a way.

"Mmm. Different." She smiled, then tiptoed her fingers along his lapel. "And you wore the tux?"

"Figured I had to go all out to impress you."

Parris shook her head. "You don't have to do that at all. You impressed me from the first minute I met you. With your mind, not your looks." She took in a breath and in the space of that moment, Brad's hope returned. "I've known dozens of great-looking guys who had nothing to offer me underneath the pretty wrapping paper. You, though, are different. You have a passion for what you do. For the people you care about. Everything I fell in love with was in here." She touched his temples.

Brad reached up and grabbed her finger. "Fell in love with?"

"Yep." She grinned. "I was just a little slow to realize it."

"A little?" He matched her smile with one of his own.

"Hey, don't press your luck." She tugged him closer, using the tux for leverage. "I thought you were saving this for the awards meeting."

"Don't need it for that anymore. In fact, I don't need you anymore, either." He shook his head, smiling. The scent of the native island wildflowers drifted off of Parris's skin. Sweet and spicy. "That came out wrong. My brain seems to go dead when you're too close to me."

"Like this?" Parris brought her lips within kissing distance of his. Heat coiled between them, raising his temperature. And everything else.

"Exactly like that." Brad watched her parted, glossy pink lips. He wanted to taste her, to take her in his arms and finish everything that hadn't been completed between them. But he had invited her here to tell her something and he wanted to get the words out before he forgot them entirely.

"So, you don't need me anymore?" She gave him a flirty pout.

"Oh, I need *you*. What I meant is I don't need the makeover help."

"You never did. You were perfect without it."

He cupped her face and trailed a thumb along her lip. She opened her mouth, tasting his finger, and he nearly lost his mind. "You're the only woman I've ever known who liked me just the way I was."

"I could have done without the Squids Are Lovable Pets T-shirt, though," she said.

"It's history."

"Good. One more thing." She tugged at the tie he'd worked so hard on. "You need to lose the tux."

"I'd be happy to." His voice was low, full of the promises to come later that night. "But why?"

"Because I liked you better the other way." She

tossed the tie onto the blanket and began working on the vest. "A lot better."

"Your wish is my command, my lady," he said, his fingers meeting hers and working the buttons from the bottom up.

She paused on the last one, her fingers halfway through the task of slipping it through the hole. "Wait a minute. Why don't you need the makeover anymore? What happened with the committee?"

"I found another grant. The Kingman Foundation has agreed to support my squid research." He tipped her chin toward his. "And for that, I have you to thank."

"Me? But I didn't do anything but talk about the whale trip."

"You couldn't have been a better salesperson for what I do if you tried. A simple thank-you doesn't seem enough. I need to thank you properly." He lowered his mouth to hers.

By the time they came up for air, Parris had been thanked a hundred times over and shown a little gratitude of her own in return.

"I love you," he whispered, "just the way you are."

Her heart sang with those words. She had no doubts, only assurance that Brad meant every one of them. He was a man who kept his word, who didn't say things he didn't mean. She'd waited long enough to realize that.

"I love you, too," Parris said.

"No matter what I wear?"

"No matter what." She gave him a wide smile, then stepped back. "I have a surprise for you. It

seems a little silly now, given what you're wearing.''
Parris undid the buttons on her simple white knit
jacket and slipped it to the ground. Beneath it she
wore an I'm A Fish Fan T-shirt and a pair of tattered
denim shorts. She'd raced through all the island tourist stores searching for the T-shirt this afternoon after
she received his invitation, nearly making her late for
their rendezvous, but the effort was well worth the
delight in Brad's eyes.

"Parris Hammond, you do surprise me." He
laughed.

"I intend to keep on doing that for a very long
time." She smiled. "You've changed me, Brad
Smith. For the better." She pressed a hand to her
heart. "And maybe a little for the worse," she added
with a twinkle in her eye and a flip of the tacky shirt.

"And here I got all gussied up for you."

"Underneath it all, you're the same man."

He laughed, then in a few nimble movements, had
his white dress shirt undone. "More than you know,
Parris."

She had a quick glimpse of a Squids Make Great
Pets shirt before she surged forward into his arms.
There, everything felt perfect. They weren't a princess
and a squid hunter anymore. They were just a man
and a woman, celebrating the beginning of something
new and wonderful while the marine life gifted them
with its own soft candlelike romantic glow against the
water's edge.

Merry sat back with a sigh and let her heart come
back to its normal pace. She closed the cell phone
and allowed herself a contented smile. She'd done it

again. Her nineteenth happy ending. Two more and she'd have her own happy ending—one that didn't involve support hose and Efferdent. The end of the curse was in sight.

She'd tackled the impossible with Parris Hammond and Brad Smith. The next one, she was sure, would be a cinch.

And if it wasn't, well, she'd be breaking out her whole bag of magic tricks, including the Ouija board and Magic 8-Ball.

* * * * *

IN A FAIRY TALE WORLD...
Six reluctant couples. Five classic love stories.
One matchmaking princess.
And time is running out!
Don't miss the continuation of this magical miniseries.
ENGAGED TO THE SHEIK
by Sue Swift
Silhouette Romance 1750
Available January 2005
NIGHTTIME SWEETHEARTS
by Cara Colter
Silhouette Romance 1754
Available February 2005
TWICE A PRINCESS
by Susan Meier
Silhouette Romance 1758
Available March 2005

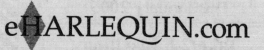

If you enjoyed what you just read,
then we've got an offer you can't resist!

Take 2 bestselling love stories FREE!

Plus get a FREE surprise gift!

Clip this page and mail it to Silhouette Reader Service™

IN U.S.A.	**IN CANADA**
3010 Walden Ave.	P.O. Box 609
P.O. Box 1867	Fort Erie, Ontario
Buffalo, N.Y. 14240-1867	L2A 5X3

YES! Please send me 2 free Silhouette Romance® novels and my free surprise gift. After receiving them, if I don't wish to receive anymore, I can return the shipping statement marked cancel. If I don't cancel, I will receive 4 brand-new novels every month, before they're available in stores! In the U.S.A., bill me at the bargain price of $3.57 plus 25¢ shipping and handling per book and applicable sales tax, if any*. In Canada, bill me at the bargain price of $4.05 plus 25¢ shipping and handling per book and applicable taxes**. That's the complete price and a savings of at least 10% off the cover prices—what a great deal! I understand that accepting the 2 free books and gift places me under no obligation ever to buy any books. I can always return a shipment and cancel at any time. Even if I never buy another book from Silhouette, the 2 free books and gift are mine to keep forever.

210 SDN DZ7L
310 SDN DZ7M

Name	(PLEASE PRINT)
Address	Apt.#
City	State/Prov. Zip/Postal Code

Not valid to current Silhouette Romance® subscribers.

Want to try two free books from another series?
Call 1-800-873-8635 or visit www.morefreebooks.com.

* Terms and prices subject to change without notice. Sales tax applicable in N.Y.
** Canadian residents will be charged applicable provincial taxes and GST.
  All orders subject to approval. Offer limited to one per household.
  ® are registered trademarks owned and used by the trademark owner and or its licensee.

SROM04R   ©2004 Harlequin Enterprises Limited

SILHOUETTE *Romance*

COMING NEXT MONTH

#1750 ENGAGED TO THE SHEIK—Sue Swift
In a Fairy Tale World...
Expert heartbreaker Selina Carrington isn't about to fall prey
to Kamar ibn Asad's legendary charm. Yet with every moment
she spends pretending to be engaged to the charismatic sheik—
romantic dinners and moonlit walks on the beach included—
she becomes more and more enchanted by his soulful eyes and
whispered promises....

#1751 THE BOSS, THE BABY AND ME—Raye Morgan
Boardroom Brides
Jodie Allman only trusts her handsome new boss as far as
she can throw him! An ancient feud between their families
makes her suspicious of Kurt McLaughlin's position with
Allman Industries. But as they get down to business, Jodie
might decide that it's time to try to mend fences with the
McLaughlins...and the sexy single dad who's captured her
heart.

#1752 THE SUBSTITUTE FIANCÉE—Rebecca Russell
Mac McKenna is marrying the wrong twin! And when Plain-
Jane Jessie Taggert stands in for her glamorous, but freaked-out
sister, sparks fly between the hunky groom and his fill-in
fiancée. What will Mac do when faced with the choice to do
his duty by one sister or follow his heart into the arms of the
other?

#1753 A RING AND A RAINBOW—Deanna Talcott
As childhood sweethearts, Hunter Starnes and Claire Dent
were inseparable. If only that had lasted! Now Hunter's back
in town to sell his family home, and he can't help but be drawn
to the one woman who made him feel complete. Maybe Claire
can help the lonely tycoon find love—and a wedding ring—at
the end of a rainbow.

SRCNM1204